VENGEANCE

JOHN LING

Copyright © 2019 by John Ling

Published by Kia Kaha Press

There is love in me the likes of which you've never seen.
There is rage in me the likes of which should never escape.

—Mary Shelley, *Frankenstein*

PART ONE

1

Maya Raines hated the idea of walking into a trap, but she decided to do it anyway.

She was dressed in a Muslim robe — long and loose and rustling in the wind. Her face was covered by a veil. She carried a grocery bag as she moved along the sidewalk, being careful not to trip on the pockmarked concrete and scattered rubble.

All around her, ominous black flags hung from the shopfronts and soared from the rooftops, declaring the rise of an Islamist *caliphate*. And just ahead, a roadblock had been set up, manned by *jihadi* fighters. A modified pickup truck — a technical — was parked on the intersection, with a machine gun mounted on its rear bed.

Maya could hear Arabic being spoken in the distance. It sounded harsh and strident; completely different to the gentle melodic rhythm of the Malay language that she was used to. These men were foreign Sunnis. They had come from as far afield as Egypt and Libya, drawn to Malaysia by the promise of killing local Shiites.

Maya felt the slow burn of anxiety in her stomach.

Sure, she could try to go through the barricade. With her Asian features and Muslim headdress, she could fool them. If she was lucky, the *jihadis* would just give her a brief glance and allow her to pass. But if not, they would stop her. And if they happened to be in a foul mood, well, things could get dicey real quick.

Maya didn't want to have to deal with that. So the only other option now was to get creative. Take a circuitous route around the block. Avoid the checkpoint entirely.

When there is doubt, there is no doubt...

It was something Papa had taught her.

So Maya veered off the footpath and ducked into a nearby alley. It offered her a tactical advantage. Not much, but she would settle for what she could get.

She didn't have the luxury of being choosy. She had no backup. No contingency plan. No convenient exfil if the situation went to shit.

The CIA and JSOC called this place the badlands. Venturing out here was referred to as 'going outside the wire'. It was so far beyond the safety of the Blue Zone in Kuala Lumpur that you had to be either crazy or stupid to attempt it.

Maya smiled a bitter smile.

Well, maybe that's what I am. Both crazy and stupid at the same time...

She was beginning to wonder if she had pushed her luck too far by coming out here. Especially when she was doing it based on the flimsiest of leads. But she just couldn't help herself. She was like a moth drawn to a flame; her obsession driving her forward.

She desperately needed answers.

She had to know for sure—

That's when her miniature Bluetooth earpiece buzzed and vibrated. She was getting an incoming call. She touched a button on her wristwatch to answer it.

It was Farah, her voice low and taunting. 'You're going in the wrong direction, my dear.'

Maya inhaled and stopped, pressing her back against a crumbling wall. She swept her gaze left and right. Farah was obviously watching her, but where? From a rooftop?

Maya spoke into her throat microphone, 'If you're seeing what I'm seeing, then you know that I was about to run into some bad company. I needed a better route.'

'There is no other route. You will need to turn around and go back.'

'What?'

'Do as I say. Go back.'

Why?

'So we can test your commitment.'

Maya scoffed. 'You want me to walk straight into the hornet's nest.'

'Exactly.'

'For your satisfaction?'

'Indeed.'

'That's insane. You're stringing me along and playing me like a fiddle. I'm sick of it.'

'You will stay the course. You will be rewarded soon enough.'

'No, listen—'

There was a click, and all Maya heard was a dead tone.

Damn it…

Maya slapped her palm against the grimy wall. She was tempted to hit redial and get Farah back on the line. But what would be the point? She had no leverage. No room to negotiate.

The irony of her situation wasn't lost on her.

Oh God. This is like Kepong all over again…

Maya resented Farah. The woman was a mole with a slippery agenda. A history of playing different sides. And during their last confrontation, a lot of innocent people had ended up dead over a twisted game of cat and mouse.

Was this just going to be a repeat?

More of the same?

There was nothing Maya wanted more than to give Farah the proverbial finger and walk away right now. But she couldn't. Her obligation to Papa wouldn't allow her to.

So, for now, all Maya could do was follow Farah's trail of dubious breadcrumbs, even if that meant going against her better instincts.

Maya rubbed her temples, groaning through her teeth. She was being manipulated, for sure. But she would allow things to run their course. After all, what the hell else was she going to do? She'd already broken all the rules by coming this far.

Might as well seal the deal…

Resigned to her fate, Maya straightened her headdress. Then, retracing her steps, she exited the alley and returned to the sidewalk.

2

Maya shuffled forward, her posture timid, her neck bent. She clutched her bag closer to her. She had to play the role of a frightened civilian, and her disguise was all part of the illusion.

Right now, that was the only thing she could rely on.

The checkpoint was just ahead.

Twenty metres and closing.

Okay. Stay calm. Stay collected. Easy does it.

Maya studied the opposition. There were four *jihadis* in total. Three of them were leaning against the barricade, and one was standing on the bed of the technical, handling the machine gun. It was a swivel-mounted .50 calibre. The kind that vaporised flesh and bone on impact.

Maya chewed on her lip.

Sweat gathered on the back of her neck.

I just need to slip past. No drama. No drama at all…

Maya reached the barrier and skirted the edge of it.

The men there barely paid her any attention at all. They were engrossed looking down at an iPad tablet that one of them was holding. It was live-streaming a soccer match with commentary in Arabic.

Qatar versus Bahrain.

Bahrain was leading 1-0 going into half-time.

The video was jerky and pixelated, the result of piggybacking off one of the few functioning Wi-Fi connections in town.

Maya was thankful for the distraction.

Yep, just keep going...

She began to feel good about this—

That's when one of the *jihadis* looked up and gave her a sideways glance. He was greasy-haired and scarecrow-thin, toting a Kalashnikov assault rifle.

Maya willed herself not to make eye contact with him. She kept him only on the periphery of her vision. But — *damn it* — somehow that didn't quite work.

The fighter turned and pointed. He spoke in English, 'Woman, wait...'

Maya pretended not to hear him, coyly inching her way past the technical.

'Hey, woman. I am talking to you...'

Maya kept her gaze fixed on the edge of the building just ahead. Maybe thirty yards. So close yet so far. If she could just get there and shimmy around that corner, she could lose this bastard.

The *jihadi* began striding towards her. 'Woman, did you not hear me? I said stop!'

Everything inside Maya screamed for her to break and run. But if that machine gun on the technical swung her way and started firing on full auto, how far would she get? She was right out in the open. No cover. No concealment. Not for thirty yards.

Fuck. Fuck. Fuck...

Cringing, Maya scooted to a stop. She kept her head downcast, submissive, like a good Muslim woman. She flexed her fingers, her shoulders stiff, like a spring coiled up to its tightest.

These *jihadi* bastards didn't know it yet, but she had already mapped out their positions and calculated all the possible lines of fire.

She knew what she needed to do.

The front of her robe was fastened by magnetic clips. It would allow her to rip open the fabric in a split-second. Beneath, she wore street clothes and a combat chest rig, along with an MP7 sub-machine gun attached to a tactical sling.

She would draw it and bring it up to bear.

It would be all about speed, surprise and violence of action.

The most immediate threat was the fighter coming towards her. She nicknamed him Alpha. He had to be eliminated first. Then she would hit the *jihadi* on the technical — Bravo — knocking the machine gun out of the equation. That would leave her clear to stitch up the remaining two *jihadis* — Charlie and Delta — still standing by the barricade, bunched up together, offering juicy targets for her sight picture.

That was the plan.

Alpha. Bravo. Charlie. Delta.

All targets triangulated for the sequential takedown.

A game of dominoes.

Maya breathed in and breathed out. Conscious of her strumming heartbeat. Felt the adrenaline spiking in her veins.

Alpha was drawing closer now, coming in at her four o'clock. She was aware of his footfalls crunching on grit, kicking up dust. The sun reflected off the barrel of the machine gun on the technical, which thankfully wasn't aimed her way just yet. The chatter and cheering of the soccer match still played on the iPad.

Everything felt hyperreal; magnified.

Maya pivoted ever so slowly, shifting her body into a bladed stance to reduce her profile. She cocked her head, watching Alpha through tunnelled vision.

Timing was everything.

She was already imagining how she would go for a killshot, drilling him right between the eyes. She wouldn't miss. Not at this distance.

Her skin was tingling.

Her muscles were loosening.

Maya was ready to unleash hell.

But — *whoa, whoa* — she stopped herself. Just about managed to ease back on her intended aggression. Because she spotted a change in Alpha's body language. He had casually slung his weapon over his shoulder, and he was strolling towards her, his expression carefree, almost arrogant.

It was obvious that he didn't see her as a threat.

He wasn't hostile.

At least not yet.

Alpha jabbed his finger in her direction, more annoyed than angry. 'Woman, I apologise if I frightened you. But we are hungry. We have been guarding this post since dawn. You have just come from the marketplace, no? Do you have some food on you?'

Maya blinked and swallowed. That disconnect in the moment threw her, but only for an instant. She improvised. 'Sorry. My English no good. Sorry.' She repeated the phrase in Malay.

The man snorted. 'I speak no Malay. We will make do with English.'

Maya nodded, her face flushed. She faked a giggle. Slowly, very slowly, she held her grocery bag open. 'Please, sir. Take what you want.'

The man took a look and pulled out two plump mangos. He grunted his approval. 'I have money. I am willing to pay.'

'Thank you. *Terima Kasih.*'

The man pressed *ringgit* notes into her hands. 'Be gone, woman.' He waved her off, his gesture dismissive.

Maya bowed demurely, then turned and continued on her way. She was clenching her jaw so hard that it hurt. Her disguise had held up, but still, she was flustered.

It was too damn close for comfort.

Needless drama…

Once Maya had glided past the corner of the building ahead, her earpiece buzzed. She took the call. 'Enjoyed the show?'

'You did well,' Farah said. 'Better than expected.'

'Save it. Where do I go next?'

3

Once upon a time, Rawang had been a prosperous town. Industrial manufacturing supported by oil palm plantations. A mix of the urban and the rural. A place for new settlers and migrants looking for a fresh start.

Not anymore.

Today it was scarred by bullet holes and mortar craters, and the persistent stench of chemical smoke and gunpowder hung in the air.

It was ground zero for a new sectarian conflict — a religious war between Sunnis and Shiites. The fighting had been fierce this past two weeks as the two sides had fought building to building, street to street, butchering each other in close-quarters battle.

Eventually the Sunni *jihadis* had gained the upper hand, driving most of the Shiite *fedayeen* out of town.

Now Maya saw the horrific aftermath as she walked past a row of street lamps. Dead men and women were strung up high with ropes, their bodies flayed, baking in the heat, attracting flies.

This was *hudud* — uncompromising punishment for anyone who dared to resist.

As hard as it was, Maya did not look away. She owed it to the victims to stare upon their mutilated faces, searing the grisly sight into her memory for all time.

What was it that she felt?

Guilt? Shame? Rage?

This was what failed nation-building looked like.

The consequences of bad foreign policy.

That's when Papa's gravelly voice resounded in her ears, as if he was right beside her.

There's no such thing as permanent enemies, kiddo. Only permanent interests. Don't believe me? Think about it. A few generations ago, we were fighting the Germans and the Japs. We dehumanised them. Called them evil. Did everything we could to annihilate them. And afterwards? Well, lo and behold, once we had settled our argument, they saw the light and ended up becoming our best buds. Yeah, that's history for you. So who's to say that the extremists we're fighting today won't become our allies tomorrow? We just have to cut them off at the knees first and bring them to the negotiation table...

Papa's wisdom was crude but undeniable.

Everything he had foretold was coming to pass.

Once upon a time, the Sunnis were their allies. The Shiites were the enemy. You supported one side; fought the other.

But now the atmospherics weren't so clear anymore. The balance of power had suddenly shifted. It was a seismic event, like tectonic plates grinding violently against each other, overturning the traditional order of things, trying to find a new equilibrium.

You had to be a fool not to feel it.

Seemingly overnight, it appeared that the Sunnis, with their genocidal fanaticism, had become the Big Bad. And maybe — *just maybe* — the Shiites were now the lesser evil.

Maya was still coming to terms with this new reality.

What does it mean? And where do we go from here?

The answers were few and far between.

Maya shook her head, her nerves raw, as she hit the next intersection. She was glad to leave the strung-up corpses behind.

Just ahead was a *warung*. An old-fashioned café in a two-storey shoplot. The welcome smell of roasted snacks and milky beverages beckoned.

As Maya approached, she saw that there were only two men visible — an elderly patron sitting on a stool, hunched over a cup of tea, and the middle-aged proprietor, standing behind the counter, deep-frying what looked to be a dish of *pisang goreng*.

It all looked innocent enough, but Maya hesitated.

Never walk into a place you don't know how to walk out of…

She was thinking about operational security.

Ideally, she wanted to do some recon before moving in. That meant carrying out a thorough sweep of her surroundings. Identifying all the points of ingress and egress. Pre-empting the hazards.

But with Farah keeping a close watch on her, that was tough. The woman was inflexible and would never allow her to deviate from the established route.

Maya hated that feeling of being played like a puppet on strings.

But, for now at least, she had to bear with it.

The only way out of this situation is straight through…

So Maya went with the flow.

She walked right into the cafe.

Both men were rheumy-eyed and gave her hollow stares as she entered. It was a look she had grown accustomed to. The expression of strangled anguish. Trying to maintain the appearance of being dignified in an undignified time.

Maya did a polite curtsy. '*Salaam alaikum.*' Peace be upon you.

'*Alaikum salaam.*' And upon you be peace. The proprietor grunted, wiping his hands on his stained apron.

Their exchange of greetings sounded ironic — almost phoney — especially given the current state of affairs in this town. But, futile as it was, it served as the best form of resistance now. Perhaps all they had.

Just then, a convoy of three technicals rumbled by on the street outside, trailing dust. The *jihadis* were cheering and whooping, black flags fluttering on their vehicles. An impromptu victory parade.

Maya watched the bastards drive past.

When they were gone, she turned back to the proprietor. 'It's a hot day today.'

'Indeed. Very hot. I am hoping it will rain.'

'Yes, may it rain and wash away all the dirt and sin.'

'*Inshallah.*'

The script was correct.

They had established their bona fides.

The old man who was the patron pushed back his chair and stood. With practised slowness, he sauntered to the rear of the shop and ascended the wooden staircase there. The steps creaked as he moved up.

'*Terima kasih.*' Maya gave the proprietor an appreciative nod before following the old man.

4

Maya couldn't shake the feeling that she was being stage-managed.

Yes, being funnelled into a choke point. Boxed in. No space to manoeuvre.

This was deliberate.

It had to be.

Here she was, exposed, vulnerable, as she climbed the stairwell, trailing the old man. The terrain was most definitely not to her advantage.

Maya wondered what awaited her on the next floor.

Farah would be there, almost certainly. But she wouldn't be alone. She'd have a comrade with her. Maybe even two. And they'd be armed and ready.

Maya considered her options, which ran from bad to worse.

Being active is always better than reactive. Do something they will never expect you to do. Yeah, go big or go home…

The old man reached the closed door at the top of the stairs. He rapped his knuckles against it twice. He paused for a moment, then knocked three more times.

The door began to open, slowly, cautiously.

This was it.

Moment of truth.

Maya felt the hot flood of adrenaline in her stomach.

She knew what she needed to do.

Speed, surprise and violence of action...

She pulled off her headdress and dropped her robe. Gripping her MP7 at the low-ready, she charged up the rest of the steps. With her free hand, she shoved the old man forward. He gasped and lurched, slamming against the door.

The hinges squealed as the door blasted back, walloping the *fedayee* on the other side. He staggered, falling on his ass, stunned.

Maya lunged over the old man, and she drove her foot into the *fedayee's* jaw, soccer-style. His head jerked back. His body went limp. He was out for the count.

Maya snapped her weapon up at the high-ready, tracking the room beyond for targets.

Farah was at her ten o'clock, and there was another *fedayee* at her twelve o'clock. He had a pistol drawn, and he was surging into a two-handed grip, starting to raise his weapon—

Maya fired two rounds at the table just beside them. The shots were suppressed, sounding like metallic taps, and the tabletop jolted and splintered from the bullet impacts.

The *fedayee* froze in mid-motion, his mouth agape.

'Lose it,' Maya said. 'There won't be another warning.'

Lips shivering, the *fedayee* looked at Farah for guidance.

Scowling, Farah gave him a reluctant nod.

He tossed his gun to the floor.

Farah sighed in frustration. She made a show of unholstering her own pistol with only two fingers before tossing it as well. 'You do make a dramatic entrance, my dear.'

'Consider it payback for messing me around at the checkpoint.'

Leaning into her weapon, Maya sidestepped, easing her way to the edge of the room. From here, she'd be able to dominate the battlespace, maximising her angle of fire, leaving no blind spots.

The old man was rising unsteadily to his feet now. The fallen *fedayee* was groaning and beginning to stir from his stupor.

Maya tipped her chin. 'Your friend's gun. Slide it over.'

The old man gave her a sour look, but he did as he was told.

That's when Maya heard timid footsteps on the staircase just beyond the doorway. The shop's proprietor was venturing up, drawn by the commotion.

'Stay away.' Maya fired at the doorframe, misting the air with plaster. The proprietor retreated.

'Miss Raines. Please.' Farah held her hands out in a placating gesture. 'There is little need for any of this…'

Maya aimed her smoking weapon at Farah. 'Oh, I think there is every need. Khadijah sent me to you. She said you would help. But all you've done so far is yank my chain and piss me off.'

'We are in a hostile territory—'

'Just because you're the enemy of my enemy does not necessarily mean you're my friend.'

'Very well. You are angry. I can see that.'

'Angry? Try enraged. I'm here for one reason and one reason only — to find, fix and finish the man who murdered my father.'

Farah raised her eyebrows. 'Mm. Our interests coincide. We want him as well. He has martyred many of our people.'

'So I've heard. The Butcher of Kajang.' Maya sucked on her teeth. 'But I have no interest in being pulled into your jihad.'

'You already are involved. Our matriarch, Khadijah, would have told you as much.'

'Enough fun and games. Where do I find Jamal Sidek?'

'Unfortunately, we do not know where he is. Not yet. This man understands that he's a target. So he's always on the move. Always roaming from safe house to safe house.'

'So you've lured me out here for nothing? It's all a dead end?'

'No, not a dead end.' Farah paused. 'Like I said, we do not have an exact fix on his bed-down location. But we are beginning to establish a pattern of life. Eventually we will have a lead…'

'You're going to share that with me right now—'

'It does not work that way. There are certain things that we need to develop. Like pieces on a chessboard. Do you understand?'

Maya scoffed. 'Quit stalling and give me what you have.'

Farah folded her arms, nostrils flaring. 'I shall. Once we come to a mutually beneficial agreement.'

'What makes you think I'll buy into that?'

'Because you are a good daughter who wants to honour her father's legacy. It is your singular obsession, is it not?'

Maya flinched, tightening her grip on her weapon, fury building at the back of her throat like acid. She could barely believe the audacity of this woman. Even with a gun to her face, she was still as slippery as a snake, trying to bargain her way into a deal—

That's when Maya heard footsteps coming from the stairwell again. She pivoted and took aim just as the café's proprietor poked his head through the doorway.

Maya was annoyed, her finger dancing just above her trigger guard. 'I told you to stay away.'

The expression on the proprietor's face was stricken. He waved his hand, whispering urgently, 'They are here! They have surrounded the shop!'

Farah grimaced. 'We have been discovered by the Wahhabis.'

'So much for hiding in plain sight,' Maya said.

'We will need to work together.'

Maya blew out a thin breath. She didn't like how the situation had just turned a full 180 degrees. But — *shit* — beggars couldn't be choosers. So she gave a reluctant nod and lowered her gun.

Farah retrieved the pistols from the floor.

The *fedayee* — the one Maya had previously kicked — stumbled to a closet at the edge of the room. He threw it open. There was a rack of Kalashnikov assault rifles. He passed them out to Farah and his comrades. They loaded their weapons in a hurry, the click-clack of magazines hitting home.

The old man joined the proprietor at the doorway. 'We will delay them as long as we can. You need to leave. Now.'

They descended the stairs.

Farah shut and locked the door. 'The roof is our only chance.'

The two *fedayeen* hustled to a window and slid it open. They climbed through and disappeared into the fire escape beyond.

Farah followed.

That's when Maya heard shouts and gunfire thundering from downstairs, followed by the sound of furniture crashing.

Not good.

Not good at all.

Things were escalating fast.

Maya allowed her MP7 to dangle by her tactical sling as she perched herself on the windowsill. And that's when she heard something else — an ominous hissing sound. It was coming from the stairwell. A whooshing crescendo.

Something in her brain — the primal reptilian part — screamed that it was danger close. But — *oh Jesus* — she wasn't through the window yet. She was half-in and half-out.

Go. Go. Go...

Maya catapulted herself forward, clumsy, lacking grace. She grabbed the ladder attached to the fire escape on her right. One-handed, she swung around, chest banging hard against the rusty steel frame.

Maya gasped.

The room behind her exploded, flame and smoke billowing from the shattered window. The rush of heat was so blistering that Maya jerked her face away, eyes watering, ears ringing. A flock of frightened pigeons took flight, brushing past her.

It was a rocket-propelled grenade.

So damn close…

Coughing, wheezing, Maya scrambled up the ladder. When she reached the final rung, Farah seized her by the hand and pulled her on to the roof.

5

The rooftop was slanted on both sides, covered by cracked tiles, sun-baked.

'We must move!' Farah urged.

Maya wiped soot from her face, fighting back nausea. More than anything, she wanted a moment to catch her breath, to gain her bearings, but there was no *fucking* time.

So she pushed herself to follow Farah's lead.

Straining for balance, she ran up one side of the roof, crested the ridge, and then descended the slope on the other side, her shoes crunching on the rattling tiles.

An adjoining building loomed, separated by a chasm.

The two *fedayeen* leapt ahead, clearing the gap, landing on the other rooftop.

Farah followed suit.

Maya was next, and she jumped and soared through the air, the side street blurring below her. She caught a glimpse of a dozen tangos swarming at ground level, and some of them were pointing up at her, yelling—

Then Maya hit the other side, knees bending, cushioning her impact, and she rolled, curling her shoulders. The momentum carried her to her feet, and she kept on running.

Sweat drenched her forehead.

Her heart was hammering.

The next rooftop was the goal.

Maya vaulted across, clearing the gap, landing, and she was determined to keep on going, her mouth gulping, her leg muscles burning—

That's when she caught a flicker of motion. It came from a shop just across the street. From a row of windows. Tangos creeping into firing positions.

'Contact left!' Maya skidded to a crouch. 'Left!' She spun and brought her weapon up, leaning into her holosight. But her posture was all wrong, and she couldn't react fast enough—

The windows exploded outward in a symphony of glass.

Bullets hissed and cracked.

One of the *fedayeen* was struck, and he reeled back, clutching his shattered throat, blood geysering. He was dead before he collapsed.

What came next was a rocket-propelled grenade, screaming through the air, leaving a wicked vapour trail in its wake.

Farah dodged left, while the surviving *fedayee* dodged right.

The rocket skipped across a gutter, drawing sparks, metal howling against metal, before it slammed into a chimney at the far end, the blast scattering bricks and granite.

More bullets rippled around Maya, dust and grit blooming. She rolled and repositioned herself behind the rooftop's ridge.

She found her sight picture and acquired her targets.

She fanned her trigger, firing controlled bursts.

The tango with the rocket launcher went down, his upper torso misting into pink.

Then she stitched up the next tango, making him dance.

Then she nailed the final tango, managing a headshot this time.

Yeah, three in a row.

Signed, sealed and delivered.

Maya reloaded, her nostrils scorched by the smell of hot metal and smoking cordite. Her aim drifted this way and that, searching for more threats—

That's when high-powered gunfire suddenly roared from the street below, and the lip of the roof right in front of her erupted into fragments. A loose piece of masonry slashed her in the cheek.

Goddamn it…

Maya lurched back, stunned by the raw power of the .50 calibre rounds.

Down below, a technical was rolling by, tyres screeching. The gunner on the rear bed was swivelling his weapon around, adjusting his aim, zeroing in on her—

That's when Farah and the *fedayee* leaned forward and opened up with their rifles, knocking the gunner clean off his perch. Then they switched up and went for the driver in the front cab, peppering the windscreen, turning it into spiderwebs. He slumped over his steering wheel, horn blaring, and the technical swerved, jumping the kerb, crashing into a lamp post.

Farah drew two grenades, pulled their pins and tossed them.

The grenades hit the street, bouncing and detonating just under the technical.

The fuel tank ignited.

Flames whooshed into a fireball.

Several tangos on the street shrieked and flailed as their bodies were set ablaze.

Maya touched her injured cheek, and she watched with grim satisfaction.

Burn, you bastards. Burn…

6

Maya, Farah and the *fedayee* kept on moving, each one taking turns to provide cover while the others leapfrogged forward.

They pushed on until they reached the next rooftop.

Safe for now.

But this was the last building on the block. Which meant no more rooftops. No more magical escape routes.

'What now?' Maya asked.

'We have a contingency. Trust me,' Farah said.

They descended the fire escape, hitting ground level, button-hooking past the corner of the building. A narrow alleyway lay beyond.

Maya swept left and right.

It looked clear, but she could hear angry shouts in Arabic.

The *jihadis* were regrouping in the main street and closing in.

Maya popped smoke grenades up and down the alley. The canisters sizzled as they released a white mist, providing camouflage. It would buy them some time, but not much.

'This way.' Farah and the *fedayee* reached down, lifting a rusty manhole cover. It squealed as they eased it to one side.

Maya went in first, sliding down the ladder into the tunnel below. She splashed into filthy water that reached up to her calves. There were rats and roaches and God knows what else down here. But she wasn't going to complain. It was either this or certain death.

Maya looked up just in time to see Farah and her comrade bid each other farewell.

'Sister,' the *fedayee* said. 'I will stay behind to distract the Wahhabis.'

'*Alhamdulillah*. We will see each other in Paradise.'

'Yes, but hopefully not too soon.'

Maya swallowed, feeling a pinprick of emotion in her heart. She didn't trust these Shiites. And yet she couldn't deny that there was something compelling about them. The way they devoted themselves to their cause. Always willing to pay the ultimate sacrifice.

It was a stirring enigma, where the puzzle pieces didn't quite fit. A culture Maya was still struggling to come to terms with. Maybe it would all make sense. Later.

Farah slid down the ladder, and the *fedayee* above replaced the manhole cover.

They were plunged into darkness.

Maya pulled a flashlight from her vest and switched it on. 'Which way?'

Farah pointed at the intersection to their left. 'There. We will keep going until we reach the end.'

7

They shuffled through the tunnel, water sloshing. The sounds of their movement echoed hollowly, their bodies bent over to accommodate the low ceiling.

The heat was stifling down here.

Maya found herself breathing through her mouth.

This wasn't the most pleasant of places.

Still, she found it to be a welcome relief from the running battle she had just experienced. This gave her the chance to slow down. To decompress. To reflect.

'Your people are brave,' Maya said. 'I respect that.'

Farah gave a low chuckle. 'Indeed. No hardship is too great for us to endure. We owe our faith to Khadijah's teachings and revelations. But you already understand that. You've met her.'

'Uh-huh.' Maya shrugged. 'She's an interesting woman. Charismatic.'

'You sound doubtful.'

'I just don't think you can fight the Sunni *jihadis* and win. You're outgunned and outnumbered. Eventually they'll bleed you dry.'

'We'll retake Rawang eventually. We are planning a counteroffensive—'

'Sure. Great. But this is just one town. What about the rest of the country?'

'We will mobilise and engage them on all fronts. And we will prevail.'

'Okay. But I just don't get how you can do it, given the obvious disparity in resources—'

'I see that you are not a believer in miracles.'

'Should I be? Divine intervention really isn't my thing.'

'For now, all you need to know is that Khadijah has guided you here under the instructions of the Almighty. *Shukur Allah.* All of this is happening for a reason. And perhaps, in due time, you will receive a blessed revelation of your own. Perhaps you might even come to believe in what we believe.'

'Which is...?'

'We want a reformed nation where every citizen will be given the right to live in fairness and dignity. No more intolerance. No more discrimination. This is what God has called us to do. And this is why we fight. To establish a better society in this land...'

Maya opened her mouth, but she hesitated and faltered. She lapsed into silence instead. She didn't know what to say in response to Farah's conviction. Well, what could she say without sounding wrong-headed? She certainly wasn't religious. Couldn't bring herself to believe in any of that spiritual mumbo jumbo.

Oh, for crying out loud...

Maya raked her fingers through her messy hair.

Right now, all she could do was cling on to reason and rationality.

She thought about everything that had led her to this point.

Months ago, she had been brought in as part of an American-led task force. Her mission? To help fight the Shiite rebellion in Malaysia and rescue Owen Caulfield, the kidnapped son of an American businessman.

Maya's team had succeeded in bringing the boy home. And there was an unexpected bonus as well — they managed to capture Khadijah, the enigmatic Shiite leader.

It was the jackpot.

But the Pyrrhic victory had come at a gruelling cost.

They managed to track down Khadijah to a hideout in the rainforest. But she was one step ahead of them all along. In a move of twisted genius, she filmed footage that apparently showed JSOC troops murdering Shiite villagers. Men, women, children. Ripped to shreds by bullets and grenades. A war crime.

It was all bullshit, of course.

A ploy intended to harm American prestige.

But, still, the optics weren't good.

So the Americans had no choice but to cut a deal with Khadijah. There would be a secret truce between Shiite forces and the Western coalition. And Khadijah's imprisonment at a black site would be kept off the books. The Americans conveniently wouldn't inform the Malaysians of this fact.

The positive result? Khadijah had kept to her side of the bargain. She had actively ceased all hostile action against Western targets. That saved lives. But, more importantly, that god-awful footage would remain hidden and hushed up. There would be no chance of a political fallout. That was just the way the White House and the Pentagon liked it.

But the negative result? The Malaysian regime still believed Khadijah was out there, scheming, plotting, fighting. And the prime minister, a paranoid tyrant, was terrified of Khadijah. Terrified that he was on the verge of being overthrown by her guerrilla army. So he had made his own unholy deal with his Saudi benefactors, bringing in foreign Islamists to do his dirty work.

So now Maya found herself in a very, very bad position.

Not long ago, she was fighting the Shiite *fedayeen* in order to support the Malaysian government. Sure, they were corrupt and repressive. But it felt like the sanest choice in a dysfunctional nation going to hell in a handbasket.

Right now, though, it seemed that the tide had turned. Sunni *jihadis* were flooding into the country. They were bringing in a toxic mix of petrodollars and fundamentalist Wahhabi doctrine. And these fanatics were in very real danger of taking over the political structure of the nation, transforming it from a mostly secular tyranny to an Islamist one.

This chilling role reversal was almost Kafkaesque. The Shiites — once the bitter enemy — now looked like the lesser evil, especially when compared to the genocidal behaviour of the Sunnis. Never mind the fact that Malaysia and Saudi Arabia were 'officially' meant to be American allies.

Up is down, and down is up. Gravity no longer has any meaning here...

This was mission creep at its worst.

They were getting dragged deeper and deeper into a quagmire.

Maya couldn't see any of this ending up well. And yet… she found herself soldiering on, cynical and weary. Doing it more out of a sense of duty than anything else.

Maya had been born in New Zealand to an American father and a Malaysian mother. And Deirdre Raines — *Mama* — had always made it a point to connect her to her ethnic roots; to anchor her. And Nathan Raines — *Papa* — had gone one step further; working clandestinely in the hope that Malaysia would take a better path, a fairer path.

It was a mission that ended up costing him dearly.

Papa had bled out in an alleyway, cradled in Maya's arms, the victim of a mysterious sniper named Jamal Sidek.

Maya recalled all of it as if it was yesterday.

The blood. The screaming. The helplessness.

It felt like *fucking* barbwire twisting in her soul, gouging deep.

She'd been a pale shadow of herself since that day, always lamenting, always obsessing.

How could she come to terms with her failure?

As an operative?

As a daughter?

Well, maybe — *hell, maybe* — this was it.

Politics be damned, this was the real reason she was here right now. To nail the son of a bitch who had murdered Papa.

Yeah, even if that meant getting into bed with the enemy.

8

It took them almost an hour to reach the end of the tunnel.

Maya felt a welcome breeze, and she saw sunlight filtering through a grated opening ahead. She heard birds calling from the swampy marshland beyond.

'Help me with this,' Farah said.

Together, they heaved the grill to one side.

Farah glided down the slimy culvert below.

Maya followed, glad to be breathing in fresh air at last.

They landed in a river. The fast-flowing water was waist-high, and they waded through the stream bed until they reached the embankment on the other end. They climbed a grassy knoll. They were on the outskirts of town now, which meant they should be safe—

That's when Maya suddenly picked up the scorched smell of *kretek*.

Cheap cigarettes.

Maya signalled Farah with a raised fist.

Together, they ducked, taking cover behind some bushes.

Just then, two *jihadis* appeared, strolling along casually, chatting in Arabic.

They were no more than ten metres away.

Chewing her lip, Maya braced her weapon against her shoulder, tracking the men. She was content to let them pass.

But — *damn it* — they stopped and lingered, studying the riverbank. They were laughing, sharing a joke.

That's when Maya heard a soft rustling in the undergrowth.

She glanced over just in time to see Farah rising slowly from her position, creeping forward, her knife drawn.

Maya felt her heart skip in disbelief.

Oh shit...

She tried to reach out and grab Farah's sleeve, intending to pull her back.

But the woman wouldn't be deterred.

There was a fire glistening in her eyes.

Primal hunger.

In a choreographed dance, Farah circled around, hugging the contours of the terrain. She was outflanking the *jihadis*. Approaching them from their blind spot.

Closer.

Closer.

Now.

Farah lunged at the nearest *jihadi*, wrapping her free arm around his forehead, snapping his head back. With a drop step, she hit his knee, and he buckled. She drove her blade straight through the side of his neck, and with a twist, she ripped his throat out through the front.

The crunch of the cartilage was sickeningly sharp.

The arterial spray was vivid red.

This wasn't like the movies.

This wasn't clean.

This was pure butchery.

As the first man gurgled and fell, the other man turned, his rifle coming up.

But Farah was already in motion, surging forward, a blur. She flipped her knife around and held it underhanded in an ice-pick grip. With her free arm, she slapped his gun barrel aside, and then she speared him right through the eyeball, sinking her blade almost to the hilt.

The man froze in place, his face contorted in a death stare. His mouth was agape, his cigarette falling from his lips. He gave a strangled moan.

Farah withdrew the blade with a wet pop, and the *jihadi* collapsed, his brain destroyed.

It was over.

Maya allowed herself to exhale slowly, her mouth feeling painfully dry. The whole execution, from start to finish, had lasted seven seconds. And in that seven seconds, Maya had caught a glimpse of exactly the kind of woman Farah was.

A *fucking* sociopath.

Unrepentant.

Unstoppable.

Farah looked at the smouldering cigarette on the ground. She stepped on it, extinguishing it, ashes floating. Then she wiped her blade clean on the tall grass. Her demeanour was calm. Her voice was even. 'This is where we must part ways. We are on the edge of town now. The danger should be minimal.'

Maya rose to her feet, dusting herself off, irritated. 'You didn't need to kill them like that. They posed no immediate threat.'

'They slaughtered my people. I aim to do the same to them.'

'You're crazy.'

Farah flashed a knowing smile. 'You had a suppressed weapon. You could have shot them and given them a clean death. Even before I acted. Why didn't you?'

Maya frowned. 'Well, maybe I don't like shooting people with their backs turned.'

'Then you have much to learn, my dear. About the nature of this war.'

'Okay. Fine. I'm a slow learner. But I'm not here to participate in your vendetta. I'm only here for Jamal Sidek. And you still haven't given me a damn thing about him—'

'When the time is right, I will provide you with the actionable intelligence that you seek.'

'How?'

'SecureDrop.'

'And I'm supposed to trust that?'

'Rest assured, we have the same enemy. Our interests coincide. *Inshallah.* All will be as it is meant to be…'

Maya could only watch as Farah walked away from the clearing.

The coppery stench of blood hung thick in the air, hideously sweet.

Insects were buzzing.

Maya hardened her jaw. She felt dirty. The kind of dirt that stained her psyche and couldn't be washed off with ease.

And — *Jesus* — despite her principles, she even found herself entertaining the thought of pumping a few rounds into Farah's spine. And why not? The woman was a dangerous animal that needed to be put down. For posterity.

But Maya hesitated, her finger dithering just outside her weapon's trigger guard, the impulse burning a hole in her gut.

This is not who I am. This is not what I do…

The moment stretched and passed.

Farah melted away into the foliage.

Now alone, Maya wiped the sweat off her face. She didn't know what the hell she had just gotten herself into. Or what it was going to end up costing her.

Somehow Friedrich Nietzsche's classic quote came to mind.

Whoever fights monsters should see to it that in the process he does not become a monster. And if you gaze long enough into an abyss, the abyss will gaze back into you…

Maya shook her head.

She looked up at the tree branches swaying above her, whistling in the breeze.

There would be plenty of time to untangle her emotions later.

For now, though, she had to get moving.

PART TWO

9

Maya made her way three klicks south, returning to a Kawasaki motorcycle that she'd left hidden in an abandoned quarry. She was glad to see that it was undisturbed, still concealed beneath camouflaged netting.

Maya uncovered the bike, straddled it and got her helmet on. She keyed the ignition, juiced the engine and departed. She took a meandering route of backroads and brush trails, doing her best to stay off the main arteries.

Her goal was to avoid any further contact with hostiles.

For the most part, her strategy worked.

That is, until late afternoon, when she ran into a platoon of Malaysian soldiers encamped in a rubber estate on the outskirts of Sungai Buloh. They were part of the uniformed army controlled by the Putrajaya government.

She could have stopped right then.

She could have shown them her Western credentials.

After all, they were supposed to be on the same side, weren't they?

But Maya couldn't bring herself to trust the bastards.

There was every chance they would just hand her over to the *jihadis*.

It's not paranoia if they're really out to get you…

So she just accelerated, tyres kicking up soil, and she went around the soldiers. One of them cursed and took a hasty potshot at her. But she just ducked her head low, compacting her shoulders, making herself as small as possible.

More shots followed, but by then, she was well out of the kill zone. She could hear the bullets hissing in the air, not snapping, which meant that the shots were going wide.

With her adrenaline surging, her fists clenched tight on the handlebars, she took a few hard turns, swerving, dodging, until she was sure that the Malaysians weren't coming after her.

Close but no cigar...

The remainder of the journey was less eventful.

No further drama.

Maya hit the highway and closed in on the Blue Zone.

It was fifteen square kilometres in the heart of Kuala Lumpur, where the rich and the powerful had consolidated themselves within a heavily defended garrison. Blastproof walls, razor wire and gun emplacements lined the perimeter.

It served as an oasis against the civil war raging on the outside.

By the time Maya approached the first checkpoint, it was past sundown, which meant that she was in violation of the enforced curfew.

Above her, an Apache helicopter gunship suddenly appeared, a looming bird of prey, its rotors purring. Maya understood the rules of engagement. The pilots had no doubt locked on to her with their thermal sights, ready to smoke-check her if she made one wrong move.

Maya took heed and eased up on her bike's throttle, slowing down.

Just ahead, a squad of soldiers from the US 10th Mountain Division manned the barricade on the road. They had their guns and spotlights aimed at her. An interpreter called out on a loudhailer, urging her in English and Malay to halt.

Turning her face away from the glare, Maya obeyed and drifted to a stop.

She allowed for a minimum safe distance of one-hundred metres.

Close enough yet far enough.

Standard operating procedure.

Despite the awkwardness of being treated like a potential suicide bomber, Maya could only shrug. This was exactly what she wanted. She planned to surrender to an American unit, as opposed to a Malaysian one.

Perfect...

Maya killed her bike's engine and dismounted. She unbuckled her helmet and dropped it. For the sake of appearances, she got on her knees and knitted her hands behind her head.

Three soldiers cautiously approached, accompanied by a bomb-sniffer dog.

'I'm friendly,' Maya said. 'I need to get to the American embassy.'

The dog gave her the once-over, and the handler signalled the all-clear. 'She's not packing any explosive ordnance.'

A soldier with sergeant's stripes eyed her suspiciously. 'Lady, we're going to need to see some ID.'

'My New Zealand passport is in my right pants pocket. Go ahead. Check it.'

They patted her down, relieved her of her weapons, and got her credentials out.

The sergeant flicked through her passport and squinted at her photo page. 'What the hell are you doing out here? You some kind of spook?'

Maya sighed. 'It's a long, long story.'

'Let me guess: all classified up the wazoo...'

'Uh-huh.' Maya rose to her feet and dusted herself off. 'Get in touch with Lucas Raynor at the embassy. He'll vouch for me.'

10

They loaded Maya's bike into the back of a Humvee, and they drove her into the Blue Zone.

Once they got past the blastproof walls and razor wire, it was like entering a different planet. The energy within was radically different from the outside.

Maya observed traffic streaming along at full tilt, largely made up of luxury brands. Mercedes and BMW and Chrysler. And well-dressed civilians prowled the sidewalks, Western and Eastern faces intermingling.

Everywhere Maya looked, shops and clubs and restaurants were all open for business. Neon and fluorescent shimmered. Music crescendoed and basslined. And, amidst it all, the Petronas Twin Towers rose up from the centre of the zone, monolithic and spiralling, visible from every direction. A potent symbol of Malaysia's oil wealth.

Looking at all of this now, you wouldn't even think that a religious war was going on.

Maya scoffed at the debauchery and the indulgence.

She could never get used to it.

They threaded their way through the boulevards and avenues, drifting away from the commercial part of the zone, moving towards the diplomatic sector.

Maya straightened in her seat as they pulled up in front of the American embassy itself. It was a tight cluster of blocky buildings, painted in a greyish hue and capped by red-tiled rooftops, guarded by staunch-faced US Marines.

Well, here we go…

11

'Goddamn it, Maya. You went rogue.'

Lucas Raynor was angry. He was so angry that his bearded face was flushed red, and with his hands on his hips, he paced back and forth across the room, his shoes thudding against the carpeted floor in an anxious tempo.

He was the CIA chief of station, the most senior spook in the country. And right now, they were meeting in the SCIF. The Sensitive Compartmented Information Facility. It was an enclosed room in the American embassy that had been purpose-built to block out sound and jam acoustic surveillance.

Raynor stopped pacing, turned and smacked his palm on the conference table to make his point. 'You can't just decide to swan over into the badlands and run your own renegade op. That's not the way this works. We have protocols. Directives...'

Maya was sitting across from him, and she was frustrated. The last thing she needed was a rebuke in the school principal's office. And she felt an argument starting to take shape on the tip of her tongue. But she just about managed to hold back the words.

Why make things worse?

So Maya chose to concede. Bow her head in appeasement. 'I'm sorry, sir...'

'Hey, sorry doesn't cut it.'

Maya exchanged furtive glances with the two other people seated at the table — Adam Larsen and Kendra Shaw. They were her colleagues from Section One. Her closest friends. They were here to offer her moral support. Not that it counted for very much.

'And you, cowboy...' Raynor fixed his stare on Adam. 'You should have stopped her.'

'Whoa, whoa. I couldn't have.' Adam raised his palms in mock defeat. 'You know Maya. She has a mind of her own. She didn't tell us she was going outside the wire—'

'I find that hard to believe.'

'It's the truth.'

'Prove it.'

'Well...' Adam hesitated, then offered a crooked grin. 'If she had told us, then we would have definitely gone with her. Backed her up. Maybe roasted a few more *jihadis*.' Adam teasingly cocked his hands into finger guns. *'Bang-bang. Boom-boom.* So, you know, the fact that we didn't attend the party means that we weren't invited.'

'What flawless logic,' Raynor said. 'This is all just fun and games to you, isn't it? Gun-fighting and door-kicking?'

Chastised, Adam's expression turned into a frown. He dropped the finger guns. 'All right. Joke made in bad taste. I apologise.'

'I'm really not in the mood for piss-poor gags. What if Maya ended up being captured or killed? Do you have any idea of what the consequences would have been?'

'Awful.'

'Try catastrophic.'

'We understand, sir.' Kendra nodded respectfully, her tone soothing. 'Officially, we're not supposed to be in contact with the Shiites at all. Because if word got out that we had backchannels with them, that would destabilise the geopolitical situation even further.'

'Correct. But let's put geopolitics aside,' Raynor said. 'All I care about is having to explain to Deirdre Raines that we lost her only daughter in action. And for what? Some unsanctioned goose chase?'

Maya fidgeted, feeling her resentment building. She decided that she could hold back no longer. She leaned forward, shoulders bunched up, cheeks pinched. 'Okay. Don't talk about me in the third-person. I'm right here.' Maya groaned. 'Look, I get it. You and my mother go way back. And you don't want to be answerable to her in the event of something horrible happening to me—'

'This is bigger than you, Maya,' Raynor said. 'This is about all the people who care about you and refuse to see you get hurt.'

'Are you trying to babysit me?'

'Damn straight. I'm duty-bound to stop you from being reckless. Have you forgotten about the blowback from Kepong and Kampung Belok already?'

Maya winced, feeling the sting of that comment. 'I haven't forgotten anything—'

'You're losing your perspective. This entire thing has barrelled out of control ever since you interrogated Khadijah. She's gotten her claws into you. Planted dangerous ideas in your head.'

'You think I'm being played...'

'Khadijah says that she has a direct line to God. But, really, she's just a wannabe prophet dying of a brain tumour. And her cult of followers? People like Farah? They're just delusional fanatics.'

'I know that already. They're all crackpots. Every. Single. One.'

'So why the hell are you so determined to shack up with Farah?'

Maya sucked in a quivering breath, struggling to maintain her composure. She couldn't believe that she was being put in a position to defend herself. Especially after everything she had contributed. Everything she had sacrificed.

But, hey, who was bothering to keep count?

What it came down to now was bureaucratic mudslinging and endless diversions.

As Maya saw it, the problem was that the American presence in Malaysia was represented by three different factions.

The CIA was the intelligence element. Spooks and analysts led by Chief Lucas Raynor. He favoured stealth.

JSOC — Joint Special Operations Command — was the military element. Delta and SEAL operators led by Lieutenant General Joseph MacFarlane. He favoured force.

The State Department was the diplomatic element. Beltway tacticians with Ivy League degrees led by Ambassador David Chang. He favoured dialogue.

All in all, it was a political minefield.

Some folks wanted to go left. Some wanted to go right. And others wanted to stick with the middle path.

It was like a stupid dance-off with terrible choreography.

No rhythm.

No synergy.

That infuriated Maya, and it was made worse by the fact that Section One wasn't allowed much input into the decision-making process at all. And why would they be? They were a small intelligence outfit based out of Auckland, New Zealand. Elite, sure, but still a junior partner in the grand scheme of things. And they were treated as such.

Maya swallowed. She rubbed her temples, steadying her nerves. 'How long have we been chasing phantom leads? Six months? And where has that gotten us? We're still no closer to finding Jamal Sidek. The man is a ghost.'

Raynor gave a weary shrug. 'His tradecraft is exceptionally good. So good, in fact, that some of our analysts believe that the Malaysians are actively protecting him. This manhunt is just leading us further down the rabbit hole.'

'And you're afraid of stepping on their toes.'

'It's not me. It's orders from Washington. We have been instructed not to antagonise the Malaysians any further.'

'So… what? You're saying that pursuing Jamal Sidek is no longer worth it?'

'I'm saying we have to consider other more pressing priorities—'

'My father served with honour and distinction!' Maya raised her voice, and she jabbed the air. 'He didn't deserve to die the way he did. Bleeding out in some filthy alley. Gunned down like he was nothing.' Maya's insides were churning with rage and grief. 'We have to get the son of the bitch who murdered him. *We have to…*' Maya's tone was desperate now, almost beseeching. 'And I won't believe that any of this is not worth it. *I can't…*'

She choked up, and she faltered. Her eyes were wet. Embarrassed, she looked away, blinking away her tears.

Everything was on the line here.

Everything…

And here she was, falling apart at the worst possible time.

She could sense Chief Raynor staring at her with a mixture of pity and disdain. And she hated that. Hated that feeling of being weak; being diminished. It was like being placed under a microscope and having all her flaws magnified.

Fuck it…

That's when Maya felt Kendra touching her elbow, reassuring her with a gentle squeeze. It was the kind of calm that only another woman could provide, given the circumstances.

'It's okay,' Kendra leaned in close and whispered in her ear. 'We'll sort this out. We will. I promise.'

Maya squeezed her armrests, her nails digging deep. She forced herself to breathe. *Breathe.* And she managed a weak nod.

Kendra cleared her throat, then turned back to face Raynor. She wore her most conciliatory smile. 'Sir, these past few months have been tough. We've all felt the stress.'

'No kidding.'

'But, for what it's worth, I actually think Farah could be useful.'

Raynor smirked. 'I'm listening.'

'Farah is a Shiite mole embedded in the Malaysian Special Branch. And up until now, everything she's done has been designed to undermine the Sunni regime and benefit the Shiite insurgents. Am I right so far?'

'Yes, the atmospherics seem to bear that out.'

'So what we're really wanting to do is to preserve the status quo, don't we? That means we can't allow the Wahhabi elements to get too strong and take over the country. And that means tapping into Farah's expertise, if we can.'

'What you're suggesting goes against what the State Department wants—'

'Sir, these *jihadi* thugs are fiercely anti-Western. Once they crush the Shiites, who do you think they're going to come after next?'

Raynor fell silent, folding his arms, his eyes narrowing.

Kendra said, 'With them, it's all about bloodlust. History proves it. Do you remember what happened way back in 2000? How Al-Qaeda operatives held a summit in Kuala Lumpur? Remember how they discussed the upcoming 9/11 attacks? And how the Malaysian Special Branch mysteriously failed to set up any audio surveillance of that meeting?'

'Fine.' Raynor inhaled sharply. 'You've made your point. The Malaysians aren't exactly our bosom buddies. In fact, they're habitual liars and deceivers. Complicit in terror strikes against Western targets. Now, what does this have to do with our present situation?'

'I'm just saying we should be keeping our options open.' Kendra tilted her chin. 'Hedging our bets.'

'By using Farah to find and fix Jamal Sidek?'

'It makes sense. We want his scalp because he murdered Nathan Raines. And the Shiites want him because he's killed plenty of their *fedayeen* as well.'

'You're asking me to approve something that's not going to be popular with Ambassador Chang. He's queasy about kinetic action. Always has been.'

'Well, the ambassador doesn't have to know just yet. All we're asking for is the chance to develop Farah as an asset. We'll keep this low-key. And we'll only get execute authority when we have something solid.'

Raynor twisted his lips. He rubbed his beard, his gaze dithering. He looked up at the ceiling, then down at the table, clearly wrestling with himself. Finally he looked back up at Maya. His expression had softened somewhat. 'Very well. I will allow you Kiwis to run with this. But — let me be clear — I will permit no Agency resources to be used unless absolutely necessary. We need to keep the circle of trust small. That means you come straight to me with any leads or ideas. We will work together on developing this kill chain. Understood?'

Maya licked her dry lips, finding her voice. 'Clear as crystal. Thank you, sir. Thank you so much. You don't know how much this means to me.'

Raynor shook his head. 'Don't thank me, Maya. I'm only doing this because I served with your father in Bosnia. And, yes, you do remind me a lot of Nathan. Stubborn like a heat-seeking missile. A real pain in the ass.' He paused and gave a bitter chuckle. 'And if I can't discourage you from engaging in a personal crusade, well, at the very least, I can help steer you in the right direction. So that you don't self-destruct for nothing. God knows I owe Nathan that much...'

12

When they stepped out of the SCIF, the door slid shut behind them with a whoosh and a thunk. Like an airlock.

'Well, gee whiz, that went great.' Adam thumbed his nose. 'I mean, if you can look past the fire-and-brimstone sermon.'

Kendra said, 'The chief's a tough nut to crack. But he's being fair. We can't ask for any more than what he's given us.'

'Which is fuck-all, when you think about it.'

'Cut him some slack, why don't you? He doesn't have the easiest job in the world.'

Maya hesitated, shifting her weight from one foot to the other. 'You know, Raynor was right.'

Adam frowned. 'About…?'

'Everything. Maybe I want Jamal Sidek so badly that I've lost my way. Maybe I've even lost my mind.' Maya inhaled and rubbed the back of her neck. 'Ugh. I'm so sorry for putting you both in this position.' Maya glanced at Kendra. 'Especially you. You're engaged to be married. You should be prepping for your big day with Ryan. Not getting dragged into this mess—'

'Hey, hey, hey. Don't guilt-trip yourself, girl.' Kendra touched Maya's arm. 'There's no other place I'd rather be than right here. We're in this together.'

'Roger that,' Adam said. 'If there's ass-kicking and name-taking to be done, we'll pull it off as a team.'

'No regrets,' Kendra said.

'None at all,' Adam said.

Maya could only blink and nod in gratitude, emotion swelling in her throat.

They drifted along the hallway beyond.

Soon they came across the CIA's tactical-operations centre. It was a hive of activity. Supersized monitors were displaying everything from satellite imagery to drone feeds. Analysts were hunched over their workstations, typing furiously, speaking into their headsets.

Maya paused and watched from behind a glass partition.

All that surveillance power, painfully out of reach.

Chief Raynor had made it clear that he didn't want CIA assets being used for a side op. And Maya could understand the rationale behind it, albeit grudgingly.

Right now, Malaysia was in a crisis.

Flashpoints were erupting all across the country.

In particular, Sabah and Sarawak — the two states in Borneo — wanted to break away and form their own nation. They had grown weary of being marginalised and having their forestry and petroleum looted by the central government in Putrajaya.

Putrajaya's response was to send in paramilitary units, as well as *jihadi* irregulars, to crush the rebels and prevent the secession from going ahead.

The Americans had their hands full trying to monitor the situation.

By comparison, chasing down a single man seemed almost inconsequential; hopelessly lost amidst the tidal wave of trouble.

Damn it…

Maya raked her hand through her hair and shook her head, frustrated.

Kendra must have read Maya's expression because she said, 'Don't second-guess yourself. We'll do this the old-fashioned way. Human intelligence. If Farah is for real, then we'll put our noses to the pavement. Start sniffing hard. And sooner or later, we'll pick up the right scent.'

Maya managed a strained smile. 'I'm just worried about resources. If it's just the three of us on the ground, we might not get that far.'

'It won't just be the three of us.' Kendra tilted her head knowingly. 'I have a few friends in the neighbourhood who might be happy to participate in our little crusade.'

'Friends?'

'You'll see what I mean. Tomorrow.'

Adam said, 'Whatever it takes, we'll find and fix Jamal Sidek soon enough. And when we do, we'll make the son of a bitch pay. I can promise you that.'

13

Jamal Sidek didn't like the weather.

The tropical air was thick with humidity.

The clouds hung dark and heavy.

Not exactly the best start to the morning.

Jamal was in a Toyota SUV, riding on the passenger side. His lieutenant, Mustapha, was at the wheel, driving. The rural landscape rolled by — *kampung* villages and palm trees and rice paddies.

Under any other circumstance, it would have been an idyllic journey.

Slow. Serene. Scenic.

But not this time.

Jamal remembered how a *jihadi* brother from Indonesia had once told him that the combination of low clouds and high humidity was a health risk. It created downward pressure. So if an insurgent triggered a bomb, the effects would be twice as deadly.

Strictly speaking, Jamal wasn't sure if that was true or not. It could have been a myth dreamed up by a raw mind. Still, he had been in the business of death long enough to take heed of superstition. It was the little things that mattered. The little things that you needed to pay attention to. Just in case.

Restless, Jamal turned in his seat, peering over his shoulder at his family riding behind him.

Puteri — his wife.

Imran — his nine-year-old son.

Rania — his seven-year-old daughter.

They were all asleep, seat belts buckled, heads lolling and swaying as the SUV travelled. Their expressions were innocent; pure.

Jamal felt his heart grow heavy with regret.

The word was that the Shiites had placed a bounty on his head. For sins real and imagined. Which meant his loved ones were firmly in the crosshairs as well.

Ya Allah. I will do anything to protect them. Anything at all...

For this trip, Jamal had taken the precaution of using trunk roads only — narrow and curving as they snaked through the countryside. They dated back to the colonial era. Back when the British were in charge of the country. And in the decades since, these roads had received only basic maintenance and upkeep.

They were rough and bumpy.

Nothing like the sleek and modern highways.

But it was an inconvenience that Jamal was willing to endure. The trunk roads were less likely to be hit by the Shiite Black Widows. Or so he hoped. It was all a game of chance, was it not?

Jamal continued studying the terrain ahead.

Eyes darting, he searched for any visible mounds of soil at the side of the road. Or clumps of rubbish. Or even the odd person just standing around for no good reason at all, possibly acting as a spotter or a triggerman.

These were signs of a potential ambush.

Corners and bends were particularly dangerous, forcing the SUV to decelerate, making them more vulnerable to an attack by an improvised-explosive device.

It was at these choke points that Jamal had to be extra cautious, constantly sweeping for threats.

So far, though, so good.

Nothing had pinged his inner radar. Yet.

They still had a few hours to go before they reached their final destination.

Until then, he needed to remain vigilant. For his family's sake.

Under his breath, Jamal whispered verses from the Koran.

About strength.

About refuge.

About salvation.

Of course, he wasn't a terribly pious man. He believed more in the obvious power of ammunition than he did in the unseen mysteries of heaven. Still, the ritual gave him comfort anyway. It had been passed down to him by his father. An *uztaz*. A religious scholar.

The curiosity of the act wasn't lost on Jamal. When faced with the prospect of violence, he found himself retreating into peaceful verses. It was a contradiction. Or a hypocrisy. Depending on how one chose to look at it—

That's when Mustapha spoke, nodding in appreciation, 'You recite the scripture beautifully. Good rhythm. Reminds me of a *nashid* singer.'

Jamal shrugged and waved his hand dismissively. 'It's just an old habit.'

'A gift from your late father?'

'Among other things.'

Mustapha smiled. 'The old man would have been proud of the *mujahid* you've become.'

Jamal sighed. 'No, I think not. He would not have approved of my chosen path.'

'That surprises me, brother. You have played an important role in the Great Cleansing.'

'My father was an idealist. He hated guns and violence.'

'Truly?'

'Indeed. He did not even bother to attend my graduation from military college.'

'I'm sorry. That must have been…' Mustapha shook his head, straining to find the right words. 'Terribly hurtful.'

'My mother and my siblings came. But my father's absence left a painful void.'

'So… what did he want you to do instead?'

'Follow in his footsteps. Become a scholar.'

'Somehow, I cannot imagine you in a stuffy library, hunched over religious texts.'

'Certainly not.'

'Mm. Do you know the British author George Orwell?'

Jamal frowned. 'The *haram* author who writes about talking pigs?'

'Yes, one and the same.' Mustapha chuckled. 'Orwell once said, "People sleep peaceably in their beds at night only because rough men stand ready to do violence on their behalf."'

'Violence begets peace.' Jamal snuck a glance at his slumbering family. 'An intriguing philosophy.'

'Some people are meant to study God's work. Some are meant to preach God's work.' Mustapha paused, one hand on the steering wheel, the other hand gesturing. 'But we are different. We execute God's work. We bring it to fruition. I believe our role is the most important one of all.'

'*Inshallah.*' Jamal pursed his lips, reflecting. 'May everything we do count for something bigger than ourselves.'

'*Inshallah.*'

14

Mustapha turned off into a dirt road. Dust plumed, and wild grass slapped against the vehicle, the suspensions groaning as they bounced along the rough terrain.

Just ahead was a cluster of *angsana* trees, rising high, their thick branches and flowering leaves offering a heavy shade. Three other Toyota SUVs were parked underneath, their drivers waiting. Right on schedule. As planned.

Mustapha coasted to a stop and killed the engine.

Jamal's family was awake now.

Rania yawned, rubbing her eyes. 'Are we there yet?'

'Not yet, *sayang*.' Jamal smiled tightly and kept his voice soothing. 'We just need to change cars.'

'Why?'

Puteri kissed the girl's forehead to distract her. 'Remember what I told you? We need to be careful. There are Shiite *infidels* looking for us.'

Rania giggled. 'I'm not afraid. Uncle Mustapa and Father are strong. They will keep the Shiite monsters away.'

Mustapha chuckled. 'Indeed we will, little princess.'

Jamal drew his pistol. He eased back the slide, doing a press-check to confirm a round had been chambered.

'I want a gun too.' Imran fidgeted in his seat, craning his neck. 'I can help.'

'Stay in the car. Look after your sister and mother.'

'But—'

Jamal reached back and tousled the boy's hair playfully. 'You're a warrior. You need to stand guard. Just in case.'

Imran crossed his arms, blowing out a sulky breath. 'Very well, Father…'

With that, Jamal and Mustapha pushed their doors open and stepped out.

Birds chirped.

Insects hummed.

Jamal examined the tall grass around them. He wanted to see if the foliage sagged the wrong way when the wind blew, which was a telltale sign of hostiles lying in wait.

But nothing tripped his sixth sense.

No immediate threats.

One of the drivers approached. Jamal recognised him. His name was Ismail, and he was a good operative. They'd served together on two previous occasions.

Ismail bowed his head respectfully. 'Peace be upon you, Captain.'

'And upon you be peace.'

'We performed the usual surveillance-detection run, just as you requested.'

'Any issues?'

'None. We are black.'

'Good. We can afford no mistakes.'

'Rest assured, for your family's safety, we will spare no expense.'

Jamal glanced up, studying the tree canopy above them. The branches and leaves would mask their activity from snooping eyes. That is, if they were actually being tracked.

Jamal didn't know for sure.

Based on the intel he'd received, the Americans no longer treated him as a priority. They had apparently taken him off the list of designated Tier One targets.

Was it because they no longer saw him as a threat?

Or had they simply grown tired of the hunt?

The actual reasons were murky.

It was a blessing, certainly, but perhaps a short-lived one.

Right now, Jamal was returning to Kuala Lumpur. The epicentre of the conflict between Sunnis and Shiites. A new op awaited him. A new target. And this engagement would almost certainly raise his profile once more.

It felt like foolishness. All those months of sprinting from safe house to safe house, keeping his heat state low, observing countersurveillance measures. Just delaying the inevitable.

We are now returning to the lion's den...

The irony was bitter.

And yet... this was a direct request from the *Emir*. The military leader of the *caliphate*. Jamal could not refuse it.

Jamal gazed back at his family. Little Rania was waving at him, her cute face pressed against the tinted glass of the car's window.

Swallowing hard, Jamal waved back.

Mustapha said, 'Keeping them close to you is the right thing to do.'

'This goes against my better judgement. My family do not deserve this hardship.'

'God will protect and provide. Have faith.'

'Alhamdulilah.' Jamal nodded weakly, only half-convinced.

Ismail said, 'We need to move now. We have a timetable to keep.'

'Indeed.'

Mustapha helped Jamal transfer his family from the old SUV into a new one.

Everyone settled in and buckled up.

Then, in unison, all four vehicles departed, accelerating in different directions, dust blooming in their wake.

This was a decoy manoeuvre.

A smokescreen.

If an American drone happened to be watching, well, it wouldn't know which SUV to follow.

That made Jamal feel better about their chances.

'How long more until we get there, Father?' Rania asked.

'Soon enough, *sayang*.' Jamal forced himself to smile, even though his heart was breaking. 'Soon enough…'

It bothered Jamal that he was no longer a true believer in the Great Cleansing that he'd fought so hard to bring about. It bothered him very much.

15

Their names were Vince and Joel.

So far as Maya could tell, they were unpretentious men. Lean and tanned. Dressed in polo shirts and khaki slacks. Subdued in the way that most Israeli *sabras* were.

They wore easy postures, looking like tourists, but Maya knew better. She could sense the apex predator instincts bubbling just under the surface.

They met on a bridge that rose over a lake in Taman KLCC, a city park in the heart of the Blue Zone. The Petronas Twin Towers loomed large against the skyline, steel and glass catching the morning light.

'So... tell us.' Vince casually leaned against the bridge's railing. 'What is the state of play?'

Beside him, Joel nodded. 'What's the target package?'

Straight to the point. All business.

Maya didn't answer immediately.

Instead she did a slow scan of their surroundings. The bridge offered a tactical position that overlooked all the walkways. That made it easy to monitor all the civilians coming and going. Filter out any marked behaviour.

So far, so good.

Kendra was occupying a static post on a bench at her two o'clock, sipping on a bottle of Coke.

Meanwhile, Adam was free-roaming and moving along at her seven o'clock, snapping photos on a camera, pretending to be birdwatching.

As an added precaution, Maya wore a portable RF jammer in her waist pouch. It would serve to disrupt any illicit frequencies, blocking listening devices and recording equipment.

The team's comms, though, would continue to function with no interference. They were operating on an encrypted bandwidth, which was exempt from the effects of the jammer.

'Team Scalpel, how's our heat state?' Maya spoke into the pinhead microphone on her lapel.

'We're black,' Kendra's voice came in over Maya's earpiece.

'We're black,' Adam said.

'Copy that.' Reassured, Maya returned her gaze to Vince and Joel.

She considered the facts.

Vince and Joel were Kendra's friends from her days as a scalphunter. They were former Metsada operatives, dedicated to chasing down threats to Israel and terminating them with extreme prejudice.

If the rumours were to be believed, Vince and Joel were intimately involved in the assassination of an Iranian scientist in Bangkok. Which dealt a blow to the Islamic Republic's nuclear programme.

Then they also apparently took out a Palestinian businessman in Bandar Seri Begawan. Which undercut Hamas' attempt to acquire rocket-guidance circuitry.

Their list of greatest hits went like that.

Surgical strikes all the way.

These days, though, Vince and Joel had retired from Metsada. They worked as freelance consultants in neighbouring Singapore. Advising shipping companies on risk management.

Antipiracy. Kidnap and ransom. Plain vanilla stuff that paid well.

But in Maya's opinion, that was just an elaborate cover for what they were really doing. Chances are, they were actually forward observers for Israel, embedded to keep tabs on the civil war unfolding in Malaysia.

At the bare minimum, they were acting as *sayanim* — clandestine helpers who funnelled logistical assistance to Israeli intelligence.

Or, to stretch things further, maybe they were *katsa* — field officers actively running a network of agents and informers.

Or, hell, maybe they were still doing the odd wet job every now and then. Just not under the direct auspices of Metsada. Plausible deniability and all that.

Maya realised there was so much that she didn't know.

Which was why she had to tread carefully here.

Maya inhaled and narrowed her eyes. 'You come highly recommended by my colleague Kendra. She says you're expert manhunters.'

Joel smiled politely. 'We do what is asked of us. To the best of our ability.'

'If I pay your usual fees, along with a bonus retainer, will you commit to an unconventional op?'

'Define unconventional,' Vince said.

'We'd be doing something that our mutual ally, Uncle Sam, would rather not touch,' Maya said.

'Politically poisonous?'

'Yeah, that about sums it up.'

Vince scoffed. 'If this op aligns with our moral compass, then we care not about politics.'

Maya nodded. 'Well, then, how would you like to help me find the man who killed my father?'

Vince and Joel exchanged a sharp look, something like electricity passing through them. They exchanged a few words in Hebrew, their expressions hardening into grim determination.

Joel looked back at Maya. 'Nathan Raines was a friend of Israel. His cowardly murder must not go unavenged.'

'When do you need us to deploy?' Vince asked.

Maya exhaled, emotions raw. 'Now would be good.'

16

The team gathered in an old garage in Sentul, paid for with discretionary funds from Maya's mother, Deirdre.

It was a grimy backlot that smelled of motor oil and exhaust. It wasn't swanky, but it was functional. It would serve as their makeshift tactical-operations centre for now.

Of course, Maya still harboured doubts about going ahead with this. And maybe she even felt a bit of guilt. She was doing exactly what Chief Raynor had warned her not to do, which was execute an unsanctioned op without his knowledge.

Raynor was a family friend, and he seemed like he had his heart in the right place. But that wasn't enough. Maya badly needed action.

There was no time to stop.

Things were in motion now.

As promised, Farah had held up her end of the bargain. The woman had sent intel through SecureDrop — an encrypted platform favoured by whistle-blowers and journalists.

So Maya ushered the team around a mechanic's worktable. She opened her laptop and set it down. 'Ladies and gentlemen, we have a target package.' Maya hit the touchpad, and a face appeared on the screen. 'Here's our person of interest. Omar Badawi. Malaysian national. He works for the Al-Rajhi Bank, the Islamic institution of choice for Wahhabi extremists.'

Joel nodded. 'We are familiar with him.'

Maya cocked her head sideways. 'You are?'

'He's a fixer,' Vince said. 'He keeps the funds flowing between the bank and the Sunni *jihadists*. So that the killing can continue.'

Adam cleared his throat. 'Let me guess: you were developing him as a target.'

Vince shrugged. 'Just keeping our options open. Nothing concrete.'

'Uh-huh. Do not pass 'Go'. Do not collect two-hundred dollars…'

Vince sucked on his teeth but said nothing more.

There was an undercurrent of tension in the air. Clearly, Adam was at odds with the Israelis. Given their past experiences, that was to be expected.

Still, Maya didn't want to have to deal with it. Not right now. So she gave him an admonishing look and shook her head ever so slightly.

Adam sighed and folded his arms, getting the message.

'Let's get back on track,' Kendra said. 'Now, I'm assuming that Badawi is going to lead us to Jamal Sidek?'

'We're operating under that assumption,' Maya said. 'Farah is adamant that Badawi is the person directly responsible for the safe houses that Sidek has been using.'

'Acting as a coordinator?'

'High level.'

'And Farah can't get to Badawi because he's in the Blue Zone.'

'Not without raising her own heat state. And not without making one hell of a mess in the process.'

Adam scoffed. 'He's just one man. How hard could it be?'

'Problem is, he's not just one man,' Maya said. 'He has close protection. Ravenwood contractors.'

'Fuck me. Not these clowns again.'

'Afraid so…'

Ravenwood was a private-military company with shady dealings and split loyalties. Maya and Adam had clashed with these mercenaries before, during the search for Robert Caulfield's kidnapped son. Encountering them again wasn't something that Maya was thrilled about, but there was no other way through this. It had to be done.

Maya chewed her lip and nodded. 'On the flipside, though, Farah was kind enough to give us a pattern of life on Badawi. Which means that we have a lock on where he's going to be tonight. We have a vulnerability to exploit.'

'A snatch and grab.' Joel smiled, rubbing his hands together. 'My kind of operation. I like it.'

'Appreciate your enthusiasm,' Maya said. 'Because we'll only have one chance at pulling this off. Let's get it right.'

17

The team scattered to different corners of the garage to prepare for tonight's op.

Maya stood at a workbench, doing a full functions check on their comms equipment.

That's when Adam came up to her. He put his hand on the small of her back. 'How are you holding up?'

Maya didn't take her eyes off the microphones and earpieces she was testing. 'I'm good.'

'So… I'm assuming we won't be telling Chief Raynor about our new recruits.' Adam half-turned, tipping his chin. Behind him, Vince and Joel were servicing the vans parked at the far wall of the garage. 'Because this goes way beyond just developing a kill chain.'

'Raynor wouldn't spare us any Agency assets,' Maya said. 'So we're freezing him out.'

'Okay…'

'Just for now. At least until we can figure out where this rabbit hole leads.'

'Fair enough. But I'm concerned about Vince and Joel. They're former Metsada.' Adam paused. 'Or maybe they're active Metsada. Either way, it's a prickly issue.'

'For you, maybe.'

'For all of us. We can't forget what happened in Christchurch…'

Maya knew exactly what Adam was talking about.

She considered it.

Back in 2011, the New Zealand city of Christchurch was rocked by an earthquake. It happened at lunchtime on a weekday, which meant that the casualties were horrific. Those people who weren't killed outright by collapsing buildings were trapped by the rubble.

In the aftermath, several nations offered to send emergency-response teams to help. New Zealand accepted gratefully. They organised quickly, setting up a search grid in the disaster zone, and work got underway.

The different nationalities seemed to operate well together. Progress was excellent.

Survivors were recovered from the rubble.

And that's when things got weird real quick.

On day three, the Israeli team strayed outside their assigned parameters, apparently entering abandoned homes and office buildings without authorisation.

When they were discovered by the eagle-eyed British team, the Israelis claimed ignorance. They said they had gotten confused by the layout of the search grid. Took a wrong turn.

But the logic didn't really add up.

The Israeli team weren't newbies. They were professionals who had handled disaster zones before, all around the globe. Why should this one be any different?

The suspicion was that the Israeli team were on some sort of illegal trawling mission. Looking to acquire and clone New Zealand passports amidst the chaos of the quake.

This was a potential problem.

Because Metsada already had a history of such subterfuge.

For example, in 2010, Mahmoud Al-Mabhouh, a Palestinian militant leader, was executed in his Dubai hotel room by Israeli operators using Australian passports.

When the headlines hit, the public fallout proved to be extremely embarrassing for the Australian government.

Naturally enough, across the Tasman, the New Zealand government was nervous that something similar might befall them.

So, in Christchurch, the Israeli team was quietly taken aside. They were searched and questioned. But nothing incriminating was ever found on them. So they were allowed to return home to Tel Aviv with nothing more but a mild diplomatic rebuke.

Maya shook her head.

There was lingering bad blood between the New Zealand and Israeli intelligence services. Mutual distrust.

But she couldn't care less about political games.

Right now, what mattered most was what was in front of her.

Maya inhaled. Gave Adam a sideways glance. 'Look, this is a black-bag op. High-speed, low-drag. And no one is as good at pulling off this sort of thing as the Israelis. They have real-world experience. Street level. That's what counts. Everything else...' Maya hesitated. *'Goddamn it.* Everything else, we can deal with later.'

'Hey, I worry about you,' Adam said. 'Your head hasn't been in the right space ever since this whole manhunt started.'

'I'm fine. I'm managing.'

'You don't look fine. In fact, you look like a pressure cooker about to blow at any moment...'

Maya and Adam had an on-again, off-again relationship. Given the stress and adrenaline of the job, it was mostly off. Still, one of the perks of their partnership was their ability to be honest with each other. Sometimes brutally so.

Maya groaned. She wiped perspiration from her face, leaning against the workbench, head bowed. 'Did I ever tell you about this bad dream I had recently?'

'No.' Adam frowned. 'What dream?'

'It goes like this. I'm a kid again, and I'm with Papa on my first ever hunting trip. We're tramping up the Kaimai Ranges. It's an adventure, and it's awfully vivid. I can smell the fresh scent of the forest pine. I can feel the mountain wind blowing against my skin. The soil and moss squishing under my boots.' Maya smiled a wistful smile, and she gestured, drawing broad shapes with her hands. 'We're stalking red deer, tracking the hoofmarks in the ground, checking the broken foliage. The usual fieldcraft. It's a long and hard trek, but eventually we come across a buck in late afternoon. It's a big boy, and he's just grazing in the valley below us. I shoulder my rifle, leaning into my scope. Papa's acting as my spotter. I'm excited and nervous. More than a little freaked out. Because, hey, it's my first time.' Maya shrugged and puffed her cheeks and gave a small laugh. 'I zoom in on the buck, and he's beautiful. I mean, glorious antlers. The kind that you usually only see in a David Attenborough documentary. Picture-perfect. So, yeah, I badly want that as my hunting trophy. Papa knows it, and he's giving me his encouragement. *"One shot, one kill."* That's what he says. *"Squeeze the trigger, don't pull."* So I measure my breaths. Keep my posture steady. I squeeze the trigger in between heartbeats. *Boom!* The buck staggers and goes down. I've done it. My first kill. I'm squealing in delight and doing a little dance. But you know what? When I get over that sense of accomplishment and look again, somehow, the fallen buck has vanished from the valley floor. Like, just evaporated.' Maya snapped her fingers, blinking hard. 'Where did it go? I'm confused as hell, so I turn to Papa for guidance. But Papa isn't there. Instead it's the undead buck that's somehow standing beside me, like some zombie magic trick, and it's staring at me with those dark eyes, panting its hot breath. I'm terrified. And I stumble back, dropping my rifle, jerking my head around. And I see that it's Papa who's lying down there on the valley floor, all bloody and broken, with a big gaping hole in his chest. Somehow...

Somehow I've shot Papa instead of that buck.' Maya swallowed, digging her nails into her palms. 'And… that's it. That's how the crazy dream ends. That's when I wake up.'

'I'm so sorry.' Adam stared at Maya, his expression drawn tight. 'I had no idea.'

'You're going to tell me not to blame myself.'

'You shouldn't. Not for something that wasn't your fault.' Adam sighed. 'But I know that you do anyway.'

'You want to go all Sigmund Freud on me?'

'More like Carl Jung.'

'As if that's going to help.'

'It might.'

'I don't need you to psychoanalyse me.' Maya straightened and pushed away from the workbench. Her nostrils flared. 'What I need is for you to help me get the right target in my gunsights. That's the only thing that matters right now. No excuses. No diversions. Understood?'

'Okay.' Adam nodded, flexing his jaw. 'Understood.'

PART THREE

18

It was late afternoon when they reached their new safe house in Kajang.

The colonial-style bungalow was in a neighbourhood dominated by Sunnis. It was guarded by ten armed men, ringed by high walls, shaded by fruit trees.

Jamal Sidek got his family settled in.

That's when the argument started between husband and wife.

'Why can't you stay with us?' Puteri's eyes were glistening, her voice pleading.

'I have to perform my duty for the *Emir*.' Jamal sighed as he cupped her chin, trying to soothe her. 'It will be brief, and when it's over—'

'*When?* When will it be over?'

'Just one night. Two at the most.'

'Can you promise me that this will be your last assignment?'

Jamal opened his mouth, his lips furrowing. He faltered in his response. So he just shook his head. He knew better than to lie.

Puteri pulled away from him and sank down on the sofa. She smoothed her hands demurely over her skirt, her face pinched. 'I have been a good wife. I have always supported you.'

'I never said otherwise.'

'But this is too much. Our children cannot bear it. Running from place to place. Always in fear.'

'Imran and Rania are strong.'

'They are hurting inside, even if they do not show it. As a father, you must know this.'

Jamal stiffened.

Her words felt like a poisonous dagger in his heart.

Yet… what she said was true.

Frustrated, he turned to gaze out the living room window.

Outside, in the courtyard, Mustapha was playing soccer with Imran and Rania, showing the young ones how to dribble the ball. Their laughter pealed.

This was a good place.

A calm place.

A safe haven.

But for how long? A week? Two at the most?

Jamal couldn't shake off that sense of foreboding.

Every time his family settled into a place, every time they found a measure of happiness, fate would cruelly intervene. They would be forced to flee, with their enemies snapping at their heels like demons. It was as sad as it was predictable.

As a result, they had no stability; no permanent abode; no home to call their own.

It was a loathsome cycle.

Run. Hide. Repeat…

It was a maddening existence, and Jamal had grown weary of it. Now, more than ever, he was tempted to give up his profession. Withdraw from the war altogether.

Yes, maybe he could move his family to Singapore. Or even Thailand. There were methods of tradecraft he could employ. False documentation. Bribes of passage. Smuggling routes.

Jamal had been thinking about it carefully these past few months.

What would it be like to have an ordinary life? A school where the children could have a fixed schedule with regular friends? To never have to look over their shoulders and worry?

It was a beautiful dream, but tragically, it was probably out of reach.

As always, what stopped Jamal from actually organising an escape was the lingering question of what would come after.

The Wahhabi *caliphate* demanded absolute devotion from its followers. It was a complete way of life. No compromises.

This was especially true of the foreign Arabs who had come to Malaysia. They were theocratic to the extreme. Fanatical in a way that Jamal had never encountered before. Their hunger for blood knew no bounds.

In their eyes, a *mujahid* losing his faith and abandoning the cause would be seen as an act of betrayal. If Jamal went down that road, he would be branded an apostate, and he would be marked for death.

No, not just me. My family…

Balling his fists, Jamal took small breaths, anguish constricting his throat.

It was bad enough with the Shiite assassins chasing him down. Did he really want to invite Sunni retribution as well?

Ya Allah. I am trapped. We are all trapped…

Reluctantly, Jamal turned back to face his wife, willing himself to smile, his cheeks twitching. 'I will try to make this my last field assignment.' Jamal paused. 'There are other ways to serve the Great Cleansing.'

Puteri rose from the sofa and embraced her husband, pressing her head against his chest. 'Make it so. For our children's sake.'

Jamal grimaced as he breathed in his wife's scent, rocking her back and forth.

He was not in the habit of making promises he couldn't keep.

19

After an early dinner, Jamal helped Mustapha to load gear into a Nissan sedan parked at the rear of the house. There was still sunlight for another two hours, which meant that they could beat the curfew on the roads if they remained focused.

'You look troubled, brother.' Mustapha grunted as he lifted a duffel bag of ammunition and dropped it into the trunk.

Jamal did a final check on his disassembled sniper rifle. Then he snapped the gun case shut and slid it into the trunk. He dabbed his forehead with his sleeve. 'I have killed Shiites. I have killed Westerners. But I have never killed a fellow Sunni. And certainly not one of ours.'

'Omar Badawi is no longer a Sunni. He's abandoned our righteous path. He's an apostate now. In fact, there are whisperings that he has been supplying intelligence to the Americans.'

'This is a rumour.'

'It's a persuasive rumour.'

'Mm. So you say.'

Mustapha sighed. 'I understand that you have your doubts—'

Jamal shook his head. 'He is the reason why my family and I are still alive. He helped us while we were on the run. He organised all our safe houses.'

'I admire your sense of loyalty. But he's a changed man now. He indulges in *haram* activities. Alcohol. Gambling. Women…'

'Yes, the nightclub that he owns is problematic.'

'It's a place of sin.'

'So we have to make an example of him.'

'Indeed. His mockery cannot be allowed to continue.'

'Of course.' Jamal twisted his lips and lifted another duffel bag of ammo and loaded it into the car's trunk. 'If it has to be done, then it has to be done.'

'You need not worry.' Mustapha waved his hand dismissively. 'We have brethren embedded within the security forces. They will give us access to the Blue Zone.'

'I'm not worried about the mission.'

'What, then?'

Jamal hesitated, swallowing dryly. 'It's Puteri. She's unhappy…'

Mustapha was confused. He glanced at the house, then back at Jamal. 'She does not find the accommodation agreeable?'

'No, on the contrary, she finds it perfectly agreeable.'

'So…?'

'So she wants us to stay here permanently. No more moving. No more running.'

'This is…' Mustapha sucked in an incredulous breath. 'This may be asking for too much.'

'Is it asking for too much?' Jamal stared off into the middle distance, the rhetorical question weighing on his conscience. 'I wonder if the time has come for us to reconsider our arrangement.'

'You want to change things?'

'I need this to be my last mission. I believe there are other ways for me to serve the Great Cleansing. Away from the front lines.'

'You want a non-combat role?'

'Indeed. I am not fussy. I will take any post. Supply. Logistics. Intelligence. Anything.'

Mustapha fell silent for a moment. He rubbed his beard, his eyes crinkling. 'I wish it could be done. Truly. But it's just not possible.'

'Enlighten me.'

'Very well. The Shiites are few in number, but they fight fiercely. We are at a stalemate now. Our attrition rate is the worst that it's ever been.'

Jamal nodded weakly, his disappointment burning a hole in his gut. 'So you need experienced operators like me in the field…'

'I'm sorry. Your skill set is too valuable. It's why we brought you back.'

'To turn the tide against the Shiites.'

'To exterminate them.'

'My reputation precedes me.' Jamal chuckled bitterly. 'You know what they call me? The Butcher of Kajang. I wonder if that's all that I will be known for.'

'Don't be disheartened.' Mustapha patted Jamal's shoulder and squeezed. 'Once we purify Malaysia and cleanse it of the Shiite heretics, things will change for the better. There will be peace. You will be able to spend as much time with your family as you desire.'

Jamal felt himself bristling at Mustapha's conclusion.

So neat.

So tidy.

So naïve.

Jamal stared hard at Mustapha. 'Tell me something, brother. Even if we succeed at purging all the Shiites, have you stopped to think about the conflict that will come after?'

Mustapha blinked, his face dissolving into a frown. 'What is this conflict that you speak of?'

'I'm talking about an obvious problem. We have invited foreign fighters into the country to serve alongside us. This works so long as we have a common enemy. But once that common enemy is removed, do you think the Arabs will graciously leave?'

'They must. That was our agreement.'

'Most assuredly, I can tell you that they have no intention of honouring it.'

'But… why? That's outrageous. The *Emir* would never allow that to pass. There has to be unity among the *ummah*. There has to be.'

'Unity is an illusion. We are fighting this current war to rid ourselves of the Shiites. But we will also have to prepare for another war to rid ourselves of the Arabs. Above all things, they thirst for power. They see themselves as more Islamic than we are. They think we are inferior.'

Mustapha looked away. His face was flustered. 'If what you say is true, then so be it. I will put my trust in God.'

'Even if that means waging another *jihad*?'

'What else is there left for us to do?'

Jamal gritted his teeth. He reached for the lid of the car's trunk and swung it shut with a thump. He had nothing more to say.

In his heart of hearts, he was beginning to suspect that all this talk of holy war was sacrilege. It was perverted dogma spun by corrupt men to justify their own bloodlust. And right now, Jamal's biggest regret was that his family would end up paying the ultimate price for this madness.

20

Jamal returned to the house and stepped into the study room.

He wanted to say goodbye to his son and daughter before he departed.

He found them hunched over a *Monopoly* board game.

Imran was older and more experienced. He should have been winning easily. But, no, he was generous enough to slow down.

Whenever Rania couldn't roll the dice properly, or whenever Rania couldn't understand how the cards worked, Imran would patiently guide his little sister through the process. He did so at his own detriment. So much so that he was now losing title deeds instead of gaining them.

The boy's actions filled Jamal with pride.

It made him smile.

As a father, he couldn't have asked for anything more.

Alhamdulillah…

Jamal knelt and hugged both his children. 'I have to go to work tonight.'

'Protecting us from the Shiite monsters?' Rania asked, her eyes big as saucers.

Jamal gave a reluctant nod. 'Yes, cleansing our country of our enemies.' Jamal turned and looked at Imran. 'You will take care of your mother and sister while I am gone, won't you?'

Imran puffed out his chest and gave a toothy grin. 'I will be the man of the house in your absence. You can count on me.'

Jamal laughed and tousled the boy's hair. 'Good. Remember all that I have taught you.'

'I promise to be a warrior.'

'You already are, my son. You already are.'

21

Bukit Bintang was the entertainment strip of the Blue Zone, filled with upscale bars, clubs and restaurants. All glitz and glamour and neon.

This was where people came to have a good time, free from the constraints of the religious laws that governed the rest of the country.

Forget *sharia* and *haram*.

Say hello to Gucci and Versace.

Maya stood on the crowded sidewalk outside the Celsius Club, waiting in line to be admitted by the bouncers. She was wearing an off-shoulder silk blouse with skinny jeans. A feminine look, but not overly showy.

Casually, Maya smoothed her hand through her hair.

She tilted her gaze and checked the skyline.

Sure enough, she spotted the distinctive shape of a surveillance blimp floating by. These were automated airships filled with helium, gliding along like silent sentinels. They carried a payload of sophisticated sensors.

In theory, they offered real-time collection of GEOINT. Geospatial intelligence. Which was why the authorities had deployed them all around the Blue Zone — to create a near-total security blanket.

The operative word, though, was 'near-total'.

There were blind spots that could be exploited, if you knew how to do it.

The queue in front of Maya moved, and soon enough, she was facing one of the bouncers. She showed him her fake ID. He gave it a cursory glance, then ran a handheld wand over the contours of her body.

The device beeped when it detected the cell phone in her jeans pocket.

With a shy smile, Maya pulled it out and showed it to him. The bouncer gave it the once-over, his expression bored. Then he lifted the rope line and waved her through.

As she stepped into the club, Maya keyed the pinhead microphone on her collar. 'This is Scalpel One. I'm in.'

It was only a little after ten, early by clubbing standards, but already the good times were rolling. All around her, dance music throbbed, coloured lights pulsed, and patrons jived to the rhythm.

The collective smell of cigarettes and sweat and perfume had congealed into something altogether off-putting. Not exactly her idea of a good time. But, on the plus side, all the movement and noise offered great camouflage. Hallelujah for small mercies.

Maya felt her earpiece buzz.

'Scalpel Two here,' Kendra said. 'I see you. I'm at your ten o'clock.'

Maya shifted her gaze. And, yeah, Kendra was on the dance floor, sashaying and pirouetting away. She wore a red halter dress, along with strappy heels that accentuated her figure. Coupled with her smoky make-up, she pulled off the femme fatale look pretty damn well.

'You came out from retirement for this,' Maya said. 'Playing the honeypot.'

'You should join me out here. It's fun.'

'I don't dance. Not my thing. I prefer to stay well clear and observe the local wildlife.'

'Ha. Suit yourself.' Kendra spun on her heels with a dramatic flourish before pairing up with a random guy in the crowd.

He was a greasy-haired scarecrow who couldn't believe his luck. He placed his hands on her waist a little too enthusiastically as they synched up their sultry movements.

Maya couldn't help but smirk and roll her eyes.

It was all a bit too much.

Turning away, slicing through the crowd, Maya strolled up to the bar and ordered a soda. The bartender served it up. It tasted bland and generic, and she ached for something stronger. But she had deliberately gone non-alcoholic. She needed to be prepared. Her edge needed to be sharp.

Nursing her drink, Maya did a scan of the club's layout. The ground level was plain vanilla. Where all the regular punters hung out.

The second level, though, was special. It was where the VIPs came to roost. It had a cantilevered balcony, along with private seating areas. Access upstairs was restricted. Invitation only.

That was where Maya needed to keep her eye on.

Despite the fact that he worked for Wahhabi extremists, Omar Badawi indulged in the forbidden. And the Celsius Club was his favourite haunt. He checked in at least twice a week. A predictable habit.

Maya studied the CCTV dome cameras mounted on the walls and ceilings all around her. Low-profile. Pretty standard. There was a good chance that Leviticus — a mass-surveillance algorithm used by American intelligence agencies — had backdoor access to them.

That meant facial recognition capabilities.

Big Brother personified.

It was for this reason that Maya and her team had taken the trouble of applying prosthetics to change the shape of their faces. Modifying their cheeks, noses, eyes, foreheads. Just subtle enough to throw off the artificial intelligence.

Of course, Maya felt a twinge of guilt that they had to resort to all this. They were misleading the CIA, and by extension, Chief Raynor. She never thought she'd see the day when they would be working against their American allies. But, then again, there was no other way. They didn't have the luxury of choices—

'This is Scalpel Three.' Adam's voice came over the comms net. 'I've got a visual on Green Goblin's limo. It's coming around the block.'

Maya perked up. 'Do you have an ETA?'

'Wait. It just rolled past my corner. It's out of my line of sight now—'

'Scalpel Four here,' Vince said. 'It's okay. I see the limousine. Two minutes, give or take.'

'Roger that,' Maya said. 'Break-break. Scalpel One for Scalpel Two, did you get that?'

Maya heard two clicks.

That was Kendra tapping her mic to signal her readiness.

They had devised a system for her to use when it wasn't convenient for her to talk.

One click meant no.

Two clicks meant yes.

Multiple clicks meant trouble.

That kept things clean and simple.

'It's Scalpel Five,' Joel said. 'Vehicle has entered the alleyway. Parking now. And... it looks like Green Goblin is disembarking the limo with his minders.'

This was it.

Maya drained the rest of her soda and looked up. She stared at the second level of the club, anticipation warming her muscles. She knew there was another discrete entrance at the side of the building, which fed directly into the VIP area. Badawi would be coming through that ingress soon.

Maya waited.

Yeah. Any moment now...

Eventually she saw him, a broad-shouldered figure emerging through the dim lighting. He was dressed in a three-piece Tom Ford suit. Looking very much like an Asian version of George Clooney. Accompanied by two Ravenwood minders, Badawi leaned casually against the balcony's railing, his eyes hungrily sweeping the dance floor below.

'All elements. This is Scalpel One.' Maya said. 'I have a visual on Green Goblin. Stand by to stand by.'

Adam, Vince and Joel gave their acknowledgements.

Kendra concurred with two clicks.

Maya bit her lip and took in a slow breath.

This was the moment of truth now.

She hoped their plan would work.

22

Omar Badawi had a fetish for white girls.

His tastes were very specific.

They had to have Eastern European features. High cheekbones, almond-shaped eyes, sleek jawlines. And they had to be sassy and outgoing, with great fashion sense.

This fit in perfectly with Badawi's psychological profile. He was an extrovert. A social livewire who drank hard and played hard. So, naturally enough, he was drawn to females who could match his brash energy.

Physically, it was Kendra who fit the bill closest. She was part-Slavic, which meant that she already had the right facial structure. The only thing she lacked was the almond-shaped eyes. But with a little make-up and prosthetic work, they easily sorted that out.

What was harder, though, was the mental game.

By nature, Kendra was a quiet professional who usually worked in the shadows. That meant embracing a very particular psyche. It was all about the ability to melt into a crowd. Stay invisible. Which was necessary when you were hunting down terrorists in the *souks* and back alleys of Baghdad or Kabul.

However, right now, this unusual role play called for the exact opposite. Kendra needed to be flamboyant. She needed to raise her heat state. This, of course, ran counter to everything that she had been trained to do as an operator.

It would have been all too easy for Kendra to falter in her performance here. Give in to shaky nerves. But, to her credit, she seemed to have nailed her role perfectly. Transformed herself into a social butterfly. And — *hell* — she even seemed to be enjoying herself. There wasn't a false note in her acting.

Maya was grateful for that.

Still, the question now was whether they'd gotten the mix of ingredients right. It was all about attaining the X factor — that unknown quality that determined attraction between a man and a woman.

There was no foolproof way to get that.

All they could really do was nudge things in the right direction.

Maya shook her head ever so slightly.

I hope we got it right…

Up on the balcony, Badawi was studying the sea of dancing patrons below.

Nervous, Maya strained to analyse his body language. She tried to get a read on the subliminal signals. But the semi-darkness and strobing lights didn't make it easy.

Come on. Come on…

Badawi's gaze appeared to skip right over Kendra, and he seemed to focus on another stunning woman dressed in blue. For a moment, Maya feared they'd miscalculated, and they'd have to resort to Plan B—

But then Badawi suddenly stiffened, and he pivoted back. His eyes settled on Kendra, and he watched her intently for all of ten seconds. He was grinning now, clearly mesmerised.

Maya was relieved. 'All elements. Scalpel One here. Heads-up. Green Goblin's itching for a taste. This looks promising.'

Badawi waved one of his minders over to his side. He pointed down at Kendra, his mouth moving excitedly as he gave instructions.

The minder nodded dutifully, then peeled away and made for the staircase.

Okay. Interesting...

This course of action told Maya two things.

Firstly, Badawi was an arrogant prick who thought he was untouchable in this place. He had just split his close-protection detail in half for the dumbest of reasons. He could have gotten one of his other minions — *maybe a bouncer* — to carry out the task. But he didn't, which revealed his level of hubris.

Secondly, the Ravenwood minders weren't professional enough to stand up to Badawi. Abandoning your principal to attend to some menial chore, even for a brief time, was a breach of procedure. That meant one less layer of protection.

Maya catalogued the lapses in judgment. She concluded that Badawi was a softer target than they first thought.

Maybe that'll make our job easier...

Maya tracked the minder descending the staircase. He started wading into the crowd at the dance floor.

'Scalpel Two,' Maya said. 'You're in play. Minder vectoring in at your six o'clock. He's on you in five, four, three, two, one...'

On cue, Kendra gyrated her hips and lurched back. That put her on a direct collision course with the incoming minder.

Bump...

On reflex, the minder spread his arms and caught Kendra as she tottered on her heels.

She yelped in surprise, then straightened and threw back her hair, laughing as she did. 'Oh, I'm so sorry. I'm such a putz.'

It was a spirited scene. It looked random, but really, it was a calculated move designed to endear Kendra to Badawi. After all, he liked his girls to be more than a little ditzy.

That's when the minder leaned in, and Kendra's mic picked up his apologetic words. 'Pardon me, ma'am. Can you spare a moment of your time?'

'Uh, sure.'

'Well, my boss would like to extend an invitation for you to come up to the VIP floor.'

'Your boss?'

'Yes, he really wants to meet you. That's him right there — Mr Omar Badawi.'

'*The Omar Badawi?*' Kendra gasped in disbelief, covering her mouth in a coquettish manner.

She looked up at Badawi on the balcony.

They locked eyes.

The effect was magnetic.

The delight on Badawi's face was unmistakable. He was beaming. Like he had just snagged a prized fish on his hook and was thrilled to be reeling it in.

Oh yeah. A star-struck white girl, so thrilled to be invited to meet the club's dark and dashing owner. Who would have thought?

And, just like that, the deal was sealed.

'All elements,' Maya said. 'Green Goblin has taken the bait…'

23

The minder ushered Kendra up to the VIP section.

Badawi enthusiastically took Kendra's hand and kissed it. All dapper and gracious. 'How do you do? I'm Omar.'

'My name's Inga.' Kendra did a half-bow and giggled. 'Pleased to meet your acquaintance.'

'You have a lovely accent, Inga. Eastern Europe?'

'I'm from Latvia.'

'I've visited your capital city Riga. Very historic. Very beautiful.'

'Oh, that's kind of you to say. I grew up in a small town just south of there.'

'Mmm. A country girl. I like European country girls.'

'And I like Asian men. You're all very exotic and mysterious.'

'Ah. Perhaps we can explore each other's cultures more. Now, shall we sit?'

'Yes, let's do that.'

Badawi led Kendra away from the balcony, towards one of the private seating areas.

Maya noted that the Ravenwood minders hadn't bothered to frisk Kendra at all before allowing her into the inner sanctum. Apparently, they took it for granted that she had already been checked by the bouncers at the door.

This was piss-poor operational security.

But Maya wasn't about to complain.

Because ignorance was bliss.

Right now, Kendra had an Israeli app hidden in her phone — an IMSI grabber. It would act like a miniature cell tower, causing any devices in the immediate vicinity to register with it. This would fool them into linking up with a false network, paving the way for a data intercept.

'Scalpel One for Scalpel Five,' Maya said. 'What have you got?'

'Signal is strong,' Joel said. 'I'm busting through the firewalls right now.'

'ETA?'

'Give me fifteen minutes.'

'Copy that. Break-break. Scalpel Two, keep Green Goblin engaged until further notice.'

Maya heard two clicks in response.

By now, Badawi and Kendra had slipped into a private booth, which was screened off with curtains. All Maya could see were faint silhouettes, and even then, her sight line was partially blocked by the minders standing guard just beyond the booth.

Maya imagined that Badawi would be turning on the charm offensive now. Ordering a round of drinks. Making smooth chit-chat. Getting comfortable.

Yeah, this was the dicey part. Because Badawi had a reputation for being touchy-feely. His style was to get right into your personal space. Fussing with your hair. Caressing your neck. Stroking your shoulder. Then venturing lower and bolder.

'You have really soft skin,' Badawi said. 'Smooth as silk.'

'Oh, you're making me blush,' Kendra said. 'You have such a way with words.'

'Tell me, have you ever modelled before?'

'No, never.'

'Well, you should really consider it. In fact, I can introduce you to the right people.'

'Really?'

'Yes, I could organise a photo shoot for you. That's the best way to get started in the industry. A portfolio of images with you all dolled up, wearing the latest haute couture.'

'It sounds so… thrilling. I'm flattered. But I couldn't possibly accept this. It must cost a lot—'

'Money is no object. I am generous to all my friends. I like to make them happy.'

'Aw, you're such a sweetheart. Are all Asian men as kind as you are?'

'We Asian men are always kind. We are always helpful.'

Maya couldn't help but snigger at that statement.

Uh-huh. Yeah, right. What a crock of shit…

Maya could only guess at the thoughts running through Kendra's mind right now. At best, she'd be irritated by Badawi's attempts at foreplay. At worst, she'd be burning white-hot with rage.

In another time, another place, Maya imagined that Kendra would have been glad to pump a hollow-point bullet into the bastard's skull. And why not? The guy was a sexual predator with a couple of rape accusations in his past. But in a country this corrupt, with a bad legal system, nothing had ever been done about his misdeeds.

Still, as distasteful as it was, Kendra needed to stay in character. She had to act frivolous. Hang on to Badawi's every word. Keep the happy juice flowing.

The local Malays actually had a word for this, which was *mengampu bodek*. Quite literally, it meant carrying the balls of the man you were trying to please.

It was a vulgar cultural concept that had a touch of dark humour about it. But somehow, under the circumstances, Maya didn't think that Kendra was finding it all that funny right now.

Stay frosty, girl. Stay frosty…

That's when Vince's voice suddenly chimed in Maya's ear. 'Scalpel Five for Scalpel One. I've done it. I have what we need.'

Maya raised her eyebrows and glanced at her watch. 'That was fast.'

'The jailbreak was easier than I assumed.'

'You got all the data?'

'Roger.'

'Are you sure?'

'Positive. It's all here.'

'Okay. All right.' Maya nodded slowly. She was no technical wizard. In fact, she barely qualified as a script kiddie. But she understood the basic idea behind Joel's black-hat method.

He'd piggybacked off the IMSI grabber on Kendra's device, running an exploit on the phones belonging to Badawi and his minders. Then, cracking open the root directories, he'd used his ghost network to start soaking up all the data like a sponge.

The hacking had gone through without a hitch.

Of course, Maya wouldn't know if they had intercepted anything actionable until they actually got down to analysing the data. She figured that it was a toss-up between a gold mine or a dry hole.

Either way, the detective work would have to wait.

Maya said, 'Break-break. Scalpel Two, we're moving on to the next phase. Let's get Green Goblin mobile.'

24

Maya ran through the game plan in her mind.

Kendra's immediate goal was to lure Badawi out of the club. She would suggest that they go somewhere more private. Badawi, being the hot-blooded male that he was, wouldn't be able to resist. And they would ride back to his place in his limo.

Badawi lived in Sri Mahkota, a gated community favoured by the wealthy. The architecture of the villas there was faux Mediterranean — all stucco and arches and palm trees. It was, of course, guarded by heavily armed Ravenwood contractors. Tactically speaking, it was a hardened target that would prove impossible to breach.

There was, however, an alternative.

A viable chokepoint in transit.

Just before the neighbourhood, there was a stretch of hilly road that ran for three-hundred metres. It just happened to be a surveillance blind spot.

No blimps.

No cameras.

No security.

Excellent terrain. This was where they would interdict Badawi's vehicle and hit it with an EMP grenade, which would fry all electronics and bring the car to a standstill. Then, with Kendra's assistance on the inside, they would disable Badawi's minders before performing the snatch and grab.

Speed, surprise and violence of action would be absolutely crucial.

They had to be in and out of there like a whirlwind.

Two minutes max.

Using an electromagnetic pulse did have a downside — it would almost certainly wipe out all digital data on phones, tablets and laptops. That would prevent them from performing any SSE — sensitive-site exploitation — to collect any intel at the scene. That meant they would have to rely on what Joel's hacking had already intercepted. Everything else was toast.

On the upside, though, the EMP would disable any radio-frequency tracking. Which was great. Maya knew for a fact that Ravenwood had outfitted all their clients with a subdermal microchip. It was the size of a grain of rice, and it transmitted a signal for rescuers to zero in on. Ironically, it had become popular after the Owen Caulfield kidnapping.

By neutralising this chip, Maya knew they could make Badawi disappear off the grid.

They would bring him back to their garage.

They would have a few hours to sweat him out and make him talk.

And after that?

Maya inhaled.

Well, after that, Chief Lucas Raynor and his posse of door kickers might come storming through our doors…

Maya didn't know exactly what she would do at that juncture. Going up against the full apparatus of the CIA didn't exactly fill her with warm and fuzzy feelings.

But she was confident that once Raynor got over the fact they had abducted a Malaysian citizen, he would calm down and give their intel proper consideration.

That is, if we actually get anything actionable out of this. Big if…

Puffing her cheeks, nervous, Maya returned her attention to the booth on the VIP level. She watched it intently. What came next would hinge largely on the chemistry that Kendra had built up with Badawi.

'Omar,' Kendra said. 'I really like you. You're caring and sensitive and funny.'

'And you're beautiful,' Badawi said. 'So very beautiful.'

'That's really kind of you to say. But, listen, it's getting late, and I have to go.'

'What? No. Please, stay with me…'

'You're so sweet. But I can't. I get these horrible headaches whenever I'm at a noisy club for too long. It's the bass, you know? *Thump, thump, thump.* It drives me mad after a while.'

'You poor thing. Would a massage help?'

'Right here? Now?'

'No, no. I mean, back at my house. I have a professional masseuse that I keep on a retainer. She helps me with all my aches and pains.'

'You have a personal therapist? Surely not.'

'Indeed I do.'

'You truly are full of surprises, Omar.'

'My masseuse will make you feel much better. What do you say?'

'I'm tempted… But… Oh… I don't know…'

Maya knew exactly what Kendra was doing.

She was dragging things out on purpose.

In the Malay cultural vernacular, this was called *tarik harga*. Quite literally, it meant haggling over the price of a transaction.

In this context, you never really said yes or no outright. Rather, you dropped hints and strung your mark along, increasing your desirability. Forcing your mark to sweeten the deal.

'I live in Sri Mahkota,' Badawi said. 'It's just a short ride away in my limousine.'

'I've never been up there,' Kendra said. 'It's where all the rich people live, isn't it?'

'Mm. That's right. It's the Beverly Hills of Kuala Lumpur.'

'Wow, okay. Um, yeah. I guess a tour and a massage can't hurt.'

'That's great. You won't regret it.'

'You won't take advantage of me, will you?'

'I'm a gentleman, Inga. I will take care of you like a princess…'

Maya watched the silhouettes shift in the booth, then the curtains parted. Badawi and Kendra stepped out, arms wrapped around each other, laughing like a couple of giddy teenagers.

They were leaving via the discrete exit.

'Scalpel One for Scalpel Two,' Maya said. 'Outstanding work. Break-break. All elements, Green Goblin is moving for egress…'

'Scalpel Three here,' Adam said. 'Copy that. We're already in the van. Departing for the staging point now.'

'Great. I'll follow Green Goblin's limo with my bike and maintain a visual.'

'Roger.'

'Out.'

Nodding, Maya pushed away from the bar, angling for the front of the club. Her anxiety had settled now. Crystallising into a sense of purpose. Yeah, this was it. The pieces were in place, and everything was in motion now. She was quietly confident they could pull this off—

That's when Maya bumped into a woman standing in her path. Instinctively, Maya mumbled an apology and moved around her.

But the woman sidestepped and blocked her advance.

It was bizarre and unexpected.

Maya blinked and stared at the woman's face under the strobing lights.

It was Farah, and she was smiling a crooked smile. 'Miss Raines. We meet once more…'

25

Maya flinched. *Jesus.* What are you doing here?'

Farah simply tilted her head and sighed. 'I will ignore your attempt at blasphemy.'

'Damn it. You're getting in the way of my op.' Maya tried to push past Farah.

Farah's expression was almost bored as she grasped Maya's arm and pulled her close. 'I want you to listen very carefully to what I am about to tell you.'

'Hey, I don't have time for this—'

'I said listen. In about thirty seconds, Omar Badawi is going to die.'

Maya almost choked. She couldn't believe what she was hearing. She shook her head, confused. *'How?'*

'Jamal Sidek is outside. He has the perfect sniper's perch. Perfect line of sight. Perfect angle of fire.'

Maya stiffened, her eyes widening. If Jamal was here and he was targeting Badawi, then the op was blown. Compromised.

No. No. No…

Maya reacted, tearing herself away from Farah, keying her mic. 'Scalpel Two! Abort! Threat imminent! Get Green Goblin back into the club right now!'

'It is far too late to save Badawi.' Farah wagged a finger at Maya, like an adult admonishing a wayward child. 'All you can do now is go after Jamal Sidek…'

Gasping, desperate, Maya pressed through the crowd, leaving Farah behind. 'Scalpel Two? Do you copy? I say again, threat imminent! You need to abort now!'

Maya felt like she was moving too *fucking* slow. Too many people in the way. But she kept pushing, powering forward, shouldering her way through.

She was almost at the main entrance now.

The front doors were just ahead of her—

That's when she heard the gunshot. It sounded distinct over the throbbing music — a supersonic crack that split the air.

Maya felt her stomach seize up.

Two more shots followed in quick succession.

A pause.

Then two more shots.

A plate-glass window to Maya's right suddenly exploded inward, and a bouncer crashed through, blood geysering from a chest wound, and he hit the floor back-first, skidding to a stop at the feet of a group of shrieking girls.

Everything went to hell just then.

The club erupted into panic and pandemonium.

26

Jamal Sidek cradled his sniper rifle, posture locked, controlling his breaths, willing himself to fire in between heartbeats.

He was in his element now.

Total focus.

He was on the tenth floor of a half-constructed office tower, the skeletal frame of the building devoid of walls. It was all just support beams and scaffolding, open to the night. Which was perfect.

It offered him an unobstructed view of everything down below.

And right now, his vision had tunnelled into what he saw through his scope.

Omar Badawi had just stepped out into the alley, and he had a Western woman with him, and they were flanked by his bodyguards.

But something was wrong.

The woman appeared to be distressed and wild-eyed. She was trying to yank Badawi back towards the doorway they had emerged from, but he was resisting her with an irritated expression. Frantic words were exchanged, and the bodyguards were intervening to pull the couple apart.

Jamal didn't understand what was happening.

It was some kind of lovers' tiff.

Nonetheless he knew that he had to act now.

So he centred his crosshairs on Badawi and squeezed his trigger, his shoulder absorbing the kick of the rifle's recoil, and he watched Badawi's face crater inward, his skull vaporising in a haze of red.

Then Jamal adjusted his aim, going for the bodyguards, his motion smooth as liquid, pulling on his rifle's bolt, ejecting a spent shell, cycling a fresh round.

Shoot.

Reload.

Shoot.

Reload.

The smell of cordite seared his nostrils, and his ears buzzed with the lingering echo of the gunshots and the sound of brass shells spinning and clinking.

Now, with three targets down, Jamal went for the only one left standing — the woman. But she was surprisingly quick, dive-rolling towards the doorway, her hair trailing behind her.

Jamal felt his mouth twitch. He knew that he could have taken the shot. But he hesitated for a split-second, and she was gone.

Mustapha was lying beside Jamal, acting as his spotter, studying the scene with a pair of binoculars. 'Good kill. But you missed the girl—'

Flustered, Jamal snapped back, 'She was a civilian. Irrelevant to our mission.'

Mustapha shrugged. 'No matter. We have live targets at the front of the club.'

Jamal swivelled his rifle.

Sure enough, there were several bouncers standing at the entrance, craning their necks, frozen in place, confused by the gunshots.

'We need to send a message,' Mustapha said. 'Sin will not be tolerated in our *caliphate*.'

Reluctantly, Jamal wet his lips, sucked in a long breath, and he exhaled as he fired.

27

The stampede was ferocious.

People were surging, heaving, screaming.

Someone's flailing arm smacked into Maya's jaw, and her head jerked back, and for an instant, she saw stars. Dizzy, reeling, she was swept along by the jostling crowd, and she was slammed against a wall.

Oh God…

She was being crushed.

She couldn't breathe.

Her lungs wheezed and burned.

Maya heard Adam's frantic voice in her ear. 'Sitrep. Give me a sitrep. What the hell is happening back there? Can anyone confirm?'

Kendra responded, panting hard, 'Green Goblin is down! Minders are down! We've got an active shooter!'

'*Goddamn it,*' Adam said. 'All right. Look, we're turning the van around, and we're coming back. Just sit tight.'

Groaning, sweating, Maya pushed back against the crowd. Peeling away from the wall, squirming, she desperately tried to move towards the main doorway.

But she could see that it was a hopeless endeavour.

It was jam-packed with terrified punters.

A fatal funnel.

No go…

So, changing course, Maya went for the next available exit — the shattered plate-glass window. She stumbled through it, tripping, and she hit the ground outside, landing on her palms and elbows, broken glass stabbing into her flesh.

She felt the stinging pain and cried out as she lurched to her feet, brushing off as much of the embedded fragments as she could, bleeding.

'It's Jamal Sidek.' Maya blinked hard and coughed, her eyes darting, desperately searching the surrounding rooftops. 'He's here—'

That's when another gunshot erupted like a thunderclap, and a bouncer to her left convulsed and fell. Shrieking patrons cowered on the sidewalk.

It happened fast, but Maya had caught a glimpse of the muzzle flash in her peripheral vision, and immediately, she knew where the shot had come from.

Ten o'clock.

Forty-five degree angle.

Maya was shaking with rage now. It gave her fuel, and she broke into a run, pounding the pavement, zigzagging as she did. 'I see the son of a bitch. I'm going after him.'

'Maya, no. *Don't,*' Adam said. 'You're not armed. Wait for us.'

But Maya's emotions were raw as hell, and she didn't even hear him.

She was too far gone at this point; like a shark feverishly homing in on her prey.

28

Jamal leaned away from his scope, easing his grip on his smoking weapon, lowering it.

He just watched the screaming clubbers as they fanned out on the sidewalks and the streets, cars braking and honking amidst the chaos and confusion.

Mustapha scoffed and raised his hands in exasperation. 'Why are you stopping? This is a target-rich environment. You need to continue.'

Jamal shook his head. 'I have removed Omar Badawi, as well as all security personnel. I will go no further.'

'It is not enough.'

'I did not agree to any collateral damage.'

'This is not the time to be weak—'

'Brother, too much blood has flowed.' Jamal sighed as he unloaded his rifle and started stripping it down to its individual components. 'We have achieved our objective. We need to leave now.'

Mustapha scowled, his lips shivering. He lowered his head. For a moment, it looked like he might yield to Jamal's logic. But then his shoulders tensed, his breaths grew sharp, and he drew his pistol and levelled it at Jamal.

Jamal froze. He pivoted his head and stared in disbelief. 'What is this?'

'Instructions from the *Emir*.' Mustapha's gaze was intense, fanatical. 'He warned me about your lack of faith. He warned me to watch over you. And now I can see that he was right.'

Jamal swallowed, his eyebrows furrowing. 'You... You have been informing on me to the *Emir*?'

'You have grown ungrateful.' Mustapha made a tut-tutting sound and bared his teeth. 'Do not forget that we hold your family's fate in our hands. Do not forget that with one phone call, the *Emir* can make them suffer for your sins.'

Jamal felt a chill feather its way up his spine like an icy finger. 'Please. Do not bring my family into this...'

'There are targets below. You will continue.'

'I can't—'

'*Continue!*'

Jamal was sickened by this. Nauseated. Was this what their religion had been reduced to? Killing for killing's sake? All because a Wahhabi *emir* from Saudi Arabia had deemed it so?

Reluctantly, Jamal turned back to reassemble his rifle. He thought of Puteri. He thought of Imran. He thought of Rania. And — *ya Allah* — he knew that a moral line had been crossed here.

He felt it deep in his soul; a horrible churning.

Shame mixed with fear.

He could no longer abide by it.

Enough is enough...

With his muscles coiling up and his heart pounding, Jamal pretended to lean into his rifle, pressing his eye against his scope. He pulled back on his bolt, chambering a fresh round.

Everything seemed to slow down in that moment of moments.

The wind blew, ruffling his hair.

Jamal grimaced.

Now...

Jamal swung his rifle around, and he used the barrel of his weapon to knock Mustapha's pistol off-balance.

Both weapons fired.

But both men had bladed their bodies at the same time.

Their shots went wild.

There was no time to reload, so Jamal abandoned his rifle, and he hurled himself against Mustapha, seizing his wrist, twisting it into a joint-lock.

Mustapha screamed, instinctively throwing his weight to one side to avoid his hand breaking. And they heaved wildly against each other, dancing in a circle, both struggling for leverage.

They bumped against a wheelbarrow filled with loose bricks, tipping it over, sending the bricks scattering. Then they lurched into a plasterboard partition in the middle of the room, smashing through it, dust pluming.

The pistol dropped.

It bounced and skittered.

Jamal released his hold on Mustapha and tried to scramble for the gun, but Mustapha reacted by kicking the weapon, sending it pinwheeling to the edge of the room. There was no wall on the other end, so when the gun hit the precipice, it just flew off into the night. Gone.

Now Mustapha lunged forward to press his advantage, raining down punches and elbow strikes, while Jamal raised his arms, forming a protective triangle around his head, blocking and staggering back.

29

Maya dashed across the street, tyres screeching, cars honking, panicking patrons spilling out all around her.

Her palms were bleeding, but she just tore off strips from the bottom of her blouse and wrapped them around her hands as she ran. Grimacing, she cinched the bandages tight.

'Maya, you need to wait up,' Kendra said. 'I'm still in the club. Give me time to catch up to you—'

But Maya just ignored the request and ripped her earpiece off. She knew that she had a tracker on her phone, and if her team needed to, they could zero in on her.

But — *damn it* — she couldn't stop now.

She wouldn't.

That's when she heard two more gunshots echoing.

Panting, Maya veered around an intersection, and she came up to the building she was aiming for. It was just a hollow shell of an office tower, fenced off, still under construction.

Maya threw herself against the fence at full speed, the chain-link metal rattling and wobbling under her weight, and she flipped herself up and over, dropping on the other side.

She hit the gravel path, shoes crunching.

The building's entrance was just ahead, blocked off with safety tape and plastic sheeting, but that wasn't going to stop her.

Maya hustled towards it.

That's when something weird happened.

An object whistled through the air, a blurry shape, and instinctively, Maya ducked. It brushed past her shoulder, giving her a love tap, and she recoiled.

It thumped into the soil of the berm behind her.

Spinning, she stared at it, confused.

It was a Glock pistol.

What in the hell?

She looked up, eyes flitting, then looked back down.

Cautiously, she picked up the weapon and dusted it off. She dropped the magazine, caught it with her free hand, then worked the slide and caught the ejected round.

The weapon pretty much had a full stack of ammo.

It was only missing one round.

She performed a quick functions check, then reloaded the gun.

Don't question providence…

Curling her lip, Maya hurried and ripped through the tape and sheeting on the doorway ahead, holding her newfound weapon at the low-ready.

The tenth floor.

That was her destination.

30

Jamal gasped and grunted from the close-quarters battle, flesh smacking against flesh, bone pummelling against bone. It was a mad flurry of strikes and counter-strikes, with both men dodging and weaving.

Eventually Mustapha managed to slip past Jamal's defences, grabbing him by his shirt, pulling him oI-balance, and Mustapha blasted a knee into Jamal's stomach.

Once.

Twice.

Bile scorched the back of Jamal's throat, and he retaliated with a headbutt, swiping Mustapha's chin, and they somersaulted to the floor together.

They rolled and squirmed, limbs tangled, trying to get into a superior position to choke out the other.

31

Maya had two choices: go slow and cautious, or go fast and aggressive.

She chose fast and aggressive.

She charged up the stairwell, taking two steps at once, and she used the flashlight app on her phone in short bursts, just enough to illuminate the darkest corners.

What she was doing wasn't tactically smart, but she really didn't give a damn.

She was close now.

So *fucking* close.

32

Mustapha scissored his legs around Jamal's neck, catching Jamal in a triangle choke, cutting off the blood flow in his arteries.

Jamal's face was flushed, his veins bulging, his vision dimming.

His brain was starving, and he would lose consciousness in seconds.

Frantic, desperate, Jamal only had one option left to him — rocking back in a violent motion, he lifted Mustapha's whole body and slammed him against the ground.

Again.

Again.

Again.

Eventually the chokehold loosened, and it was enough for Jamal to break free, and gasping, he scooted backwards. He was weak from his exertions, and he struggled to catch his breath.

But Mustapha was already on his feet, grabbing a loose brick from the pile close by, and with a cruel sneer, Mustapha was now coming after Jamal with murderous intent.

33

Maya reached the tenth floor, button-hooking past the stairwell's landing, and she decided to kill the glow on her phone.

It would do more harm than good at this point, and she didn't want to telegraph her movements to her enemy.

Jaw clenched, sweat dripping down her face, she gripped her gun at the high-ready, shuffling forward in a shooter's stance, head pivoting. There was just enough ambient light for her to navigate. Problem was, there was a lot of loose plastic sheeting hanging from the ceiling, flapping and wrinkling in the breeze.

More than once, she caught a flicker of motion, and she jerked her gun around to address the threat, only to find that it was a false alarm.

Goddamn it...

Nerves on edge, she drifted down a corridor, clearing one office, then clearing another—

That's when she heard it: grunting and scraping and thudding.

Frowning, she quick-stepped through the doorway ahead, pushing through a plastic sheet. Breathing through her teeth now, her heart racing, she sliced the pie, taking the corner at the widest possible angle—

There. Right there...

Ten yards away, Maya glimpsed two men locked in a furious struggle on the ground, grappling for leverage, before suddenly lunging apart.

One man rolled to his feet, snatching up what appeared to be a brick, raising it high, and he was chasing after the other man who was still on the floor, scampering backwards.

Maya couldn't see their faces clearly enough to make a positive ID.

Everything was cloaked in shadow.

So she went for the most immediate threat: the standing man. She hit him with two rounds to the chest, stopping him in his tracks. As he groaned and faltered, she fired another round into his head. The man fell, his legs folding up beneath him, and the brick thudded and cracked against the floor.

The other man on the ground flinched, his arms outstretched in a defensive posture. He turned to look at Maya. The whites of his eyes were plainly visible. His mouth was open and trembling.

Maya took a cautious step forward.

Then another.

The man still sat frozen.

She studied the contours of his features, comparing it against what she had only seen in surveillance footage and photographs. He was a little thinner than she expected, more gaunt, but it was him. Definitely him.

Jamal Sidek.

The Butcher of Kajang.

The man who had murdered her father.

Oh God…

How long had she waited for this moment?

How long had she obsessed about it?

Her shoulders were tight, and her fingers were flexing around her weapon, her bandaged palms slick with perspiration and blood.

All she had to do was squeeze.

Yeah, just squeeze.

And it would be done.

Her vengeance would be fulfilled.

And yet… there was something about Jamal's stare that gave her pause. It was unsettling enough to make the small hairs on her neck stand on end.

All this time, she had imagined him to be a ruthless killer; a religious fanatic; the ultimate personification of evil. And how she would be justified in ending his life without any hesitation or regret.

But — *damn it* — right here, right now, she was suddenly struck by how… ordinary this man appeared to be. He looked vulnerable. Small. Diminished.

Nothing like the monster she had made him out to be.

Maya felt herself agonising over this.

The *fucking* pieces just didn't fit.

Her breaths grew hitched, and her aim wavered.

I can't do it. I can't…

That's when Jamal seized the moment, vaulting to his feet, breaking into a sprint.

And that was enough to snap her out of her reverie.

Do it for Papa. Do it now…

Maya felt the anguish scorching her senses, and she couldn't contain herself any longer.

She screamed, tracking Jamal with her gun, and she fanned her trigger.

34

Jamal cowered as he ran, shielding himself from fragments of masonry flying as bullets hammered the pillar beside him. His eyes stung from the swirling dust.

He didn't understand what was happening.

Who was this woman?

Why did she seem so familiar to him?

Panting, Jamal whipped around the bend in the corridor ahead, and he ducked into an office, diving to the floor, sliding around a granite counter.

With his eyes wild, he swallowed and listened.

The woman's steps echoed.

She was searching for him.

Getting closer.

Fidgeting, Jamal wanted to make a dash for the stairwell. But, no, that wasn't going to work. This woman was cunning enough to block him off from that escape route. He'd never make it.

Twisting his lips, with his back pressed against the counter, Jamal gazed ahead at the edge of the room. This was the eastern side of the building. There was no wall here. Only open space. The night sky beckoned.

He was desperate now, trembling. All he could think about was his family. He needed to get back to them. Whatever it took.

Under his breath, he whispered verses from the Koran.

About strength.
About refuge.
About salvation.

Then, counting to three, Jamal launched himself out from behind the counter.

He darted.

That's when more gunshots erupted, and he felt a streak of pain along his left side, and the shock of it caused him to pitch forward and stagger.

He was hit.

But — *no* — he couldn't slow down.

He couldn't afford to.

Whimpering, grimacing, he clutched his wound and powered forward. He reached the precipice ahead, and with his heart seizing up in his chest, he went over the edge, embracing the abyss, going into freefall.

35

The slide on Maya's pistol locked back on empty.
She was stunned. Couldn't believe it.
The bastard had thrown himself right out of the building.
Shit. Shit. Shit…
With her breath caught in her throat, Maya rushed over to the edge and peered over.

36

With bullets chasing him, Jamal had done the only thing he could — he'd catapulted himself out into the night.

But he wasn't suicidal at all.

Only hoping against hope that his calculations were correct.

Jamal plummeted four storeys, his arms and legs windmilling, and he crashed into the safety mesh and tarpaulin covering the scaffolding below. The fabric cushioned his fall but couldn't hold his weight. And he blasted straight through, hitting the wooden floorboard directly under in a bone-jarring impact, his teeth slamming together in a starburst of pain.

The platform splintered and creaked.

But — *Alhamdulillah* — it held.

Jamal was hurting everywhere. Vertigo and nausea gripped him, and he retched and vomited all over himself.

Trembling, wiping his mouth, he glanced up. Through the ripped canvas, he could see the woman staring down at him, her expression knotted in disbelief. Her pistol looked like it was out of ammunition. But she wasn't going to stop.

She shook her head and disappeared from sight.

She would be using the stairs to come after him.

Move. You have to move now....

Jamal crawled frantically along the platform.

There was a ladder attached to the scaffolding. He threw himself against it, straddling the frame, sliding down fast, and he hit the ground level.

He tumbled, smacking his face against the gravel, tasting dirt.

With his eyes watering and his gunshot wound burning, he staggered to his feet. He hobbled to the fence just ahead. Panting, he clawed at the chain-link, making two attempts before he managed to mount it and flip himself over, dropping clumsily on the other side.

Swaying, bleeding, he veered away from the construction site, hitting an intersection, crossing the street, taking the next corner.

All around him, frightened people were running, jostling, and he could hear emergency sirens blaring. The first responders would be locking down the entire block soon enough.

He had two minutes.

Maybe less.

Which was worse? To be caught by the government security forces? Or to be chased down by the woman behind him?

Neither prospect appealed to him.

So Jamal pushed through the doors of the nearest shopfront, reeling into a restaurant. It was an American-style diner, decorated with cowboy memorabilia. The smoky smell of grilled chicken and roast potatoes hung heavy. And Kenny Rogers sang from the jukebox in the corner, offering piety wisdom about the art of gambling — when to hold them and when to fold them.

Jamal was lightheaded, woozy.

He faltered and bumped against a table, spilling blood.

A waitress gasped and cupped her mouth.

Jamal sucked in thin breaths. He steadied himself and grabbed the tablecloth, pressing it against his side, compressing his wound. He moved to the rear of the restaurant, entering the kitchen.

A cook wearing an apron tried to stop him.

But Jamal was having none of that. He just blasted his

palm into the man's face, shattering his nose, and the man tottered back, his body slamming against a stove.

Jamal stepped past the fallen man, and he found the back door. He shoved it open, and he staggered into the alley beyond.

Bracing himself against the grimy wall, he struggled to keep on moving.

He didn't have a plan.

His only objective now was to find cover and concealment—

That's when he heard an engine roaring and tyres squealing ahead of him. He jerked his gaze up, and he saw a van appearing in the mouth of the alley, cutting off his escape. Its side door rolled open, and two men leapt out, their faces covered by ski masks.

Jamal felt his heart drop.

No. No. No…

He tried to retreat.

But it was too late.

There was a hiss and a whoosh.

Jamal felt a stinging sensation in his chest, and it swelled into a wave of nausea. A thousand volts of electricity rocked him, and he fell to one knee. With his hands shaking, he tried to pull the barbs out of his chest.

But the current was too strong.

His flesh sizzled; his muscles cramped up.

He slumped to the ground, convulsing.

That's when he felt strong arms seizing him, dragging him, hustling him into the van, the door sliding shut with a thump.

'My family,' Jamal whimpered. 'Please don't hurt my family…'

That's when his consciousness blacked out.

PART FOUR

37

They had to exfiltrate in a hurry.

Problem was, the whole area was in the process of being locked down by Malaysian paramilitary units. Armoured personnel carriers were rolling in, and barricades were going up at all the main intersections.

Their window for escape was rapidly closing.

Adam was the wheelman, and Joel was in the van's passenger seat, acting as the navigator. With a ruggedised laptop on his lap, he hacked into the Malaysian radio frequencies, pinpointing exactly where the cordons were being set up.

That allowed Adam to take a haphazard detour to get around them, hitting the side streets and back lanes, veering, dodging.

That's when a low-flying Black Hawk helicopter approached, rotors purring. And Adam was forced to take cover beneath an underpass, braking hard, killing the lights.

It was a nail-biting moment, but the helo didn't linger. It just continued on its trajectory and drifted away. No doubt ferrying troops to the scene of the attack.

Adam cranked up speed again, and eventually, they were in the clear.

They were out of the Bukit Bintang district.

That's when Adam exhaled sharply and slapped his steering in elation. 'What a rollercoaster. *Shit...*'

Maya was silent as she sat at the back of the van, breathing in the pungent smell of antiseptic as Kendra cleaned and dressed her wounds.

'You just couldn't help yourself, could you?' Adam smirked and gazed at Maya through the rear-view mirror. 'You had to go into full Jack Bauer mode. Chase down the high-value target on your own. And, yeah, here we are. From the frying pan into the fire...'

Maya said nothing. She just exchanged a knowing glance with Kendra. The two women had a shared kinship; an intimate understanding of the allure of revenge. Maya knew that Kendra wouldn't judge her for what she had done, as messy as it was.

Adam scoffed. 'Our heat state is boiling red right now. You can bet that Chief Raynor is going to bring the hammer down hard on our collective asses. And it ain't gonna be pretty when that happens...'

Maya sighed.

She turned her attention to Jamal, who was lying on the floor, shackled.

Vince was tending to Jamal, using his skills as a medic to stabilise Jamal's gunshot wound with combat gauze and a tourniquet.

'How bad is it?' Maya asked.

Vince said, 'The bullet burrowed through skin and muscle. Nicked a rib. But it exited cleanly. No damage to arteries or organs. A modest injury, if anything. The rest are just bruises and scrapes.'

'Well, two cheers for Western democracy,' Kendra said. 'The son of a bitch will live to see justice.'

Maya blinked hard and took a nervous sip from a water bottle.

She stared down at the crumpled photograph on her lap. She had retrieved it from one of Jamal's pockets. It was a picture of him with his family — wife, son, daughter. They were posing at a waterfall in a rainforest somewhere, wearing cheesy smiles, making peace signs with their outstretched hands.

Maya inhaled, her forehead creasing.

This was a surreal moment.

Yes, of course, she had chased down and caught the man who had murdered her father. She should have been feeling happy. Victorious. But, no, there was none of that. Just this sickly ache in her heart of hearts.

That's when Papa's gravelly voice resounded in her ears, as if he was right beside her.

It's human nature to hate our enemies, kiddo. We dehumanise them. Call them evil. Do everything we can to obliterate them with bullets and bombs. But that's the easy part. It doesn't take much effort. Just lock and load and pull the trigger. Find, fix and finish. Like I said, easy. But do you want to know what the most difficult part is? Do you? Well, here it is: learning to empathise with our enemies. Seeing ourselves through their eyes. Understanding their frustrations and motivations. Now, pay attention to the fact that I said empathise, not sympathise. Because they're still the enemy and rightfully so. We have to fight them with everything that we've got. But if we can't even understand why they're doing what they're doing, how can we hope to defeat them? We can't break the cycle of conflict if we don't even know what the cycle is…

Maya thought about it.

Agonised over it.

She knew what Jamal had done — his ops, his methods, his kills. But, right here, right now, she was seeing another side to him.

A husband.

A father.

A family man.

And yet... she was drawing a blank when it came to his family. Up until now, she hadn't even known they existed. Jamal had apparently kept them off the radar all this time. Which was remarkable, considering the HUMINT and SIGINT surveillance packages that had been employed against him for the past six months.

Maya ran her tongue across her teeth. And for the first time in forever, she felt like she was clutching at straws, without a goddamn clue on what to do next.

38

With the glitz and glamour of Bukit Bintang firmly behind them, Adam turned into Pudu. It was a rougher and shabbier district, with narrow boulevards and decaying buildings. The ambience was distinctly working class.

They coasted to a stop beside a wet market. The skid-row shops here were shuttered and deserted, and the stench of slaughtered chicken and salty fish lingered in the air.

Just around the corner, under the orange glow of sodium-vapour streetlamps, feral dogs were digging through a pile of rubbish, fighting for scraps.

This wasn't exactly the most attractive locale in the Blue Zone.

But it was perfect because it was a surveillance blind spot.

No cameras.

No blimps.

No tails.

This was where they abandoned their vehicle and switched over to a fresh van they had parked here earlier in the evening as a contingency. Different make, different colour, false plates. It was probably overkill, but given their present circumstance, it was better to limit their exposure.

Once they did the transfer, they were on the move once more.

Maya understood that the clock was ticking now.

The CIA would be using their Leviticus algorithm to tap into all the surveillance feeds in the Bukit Bintang area. And once they crunched all the data, they would figure out what had happened. Then Chief Raynor would throw a hissy fit, shutting Maya down, forcing her to hand Jamal over to him.

A predictable outcome.

His turf, his rules.

Damn it...

On one hand, Maya wanted to just kill Jamal and be done with this fiasco. But, on the other hand, she didn't know if she could actually bring herself to do it.

Knowing that he had a family had stirred up conflicting emotions within her.

She was torn between two extremes.

Her thirst for vengeance versus her thirst for answers.

Why had Jamal emerged from hiding? Why did he kill Omar Badawi? And who was the other gunman that he was fighting with?

Questions. So many questions...

Maya raked her hands through her hair, grimacing.

For years, she had psyched herself — *yeah, brainwashed herself* — into believing that her father's killer was evil. Monstrous. But now that she was actually seeing Jamal in the flesh, her assumptions were shattered.

The truth, once so certain and rigid, was now as amorphous as quicksand.

And Maya knew — *oh God* — she knew that she had to keep Jamal alive.

At least until she could figure out what the stakes were.

39

When they returned to their garage in Sentul, they unloaded Jamal from the van.

Vince and Joel strapped him to a gurney. They used saline irrigation to flush out and clean his wound. Then they treated him with antibiotics. Then Vince started sewing him up, while Joel started hooking up an IV drip.

Maya, Kendra and Adam stood back, watching Vince and Joel work.

Adam sighed and rubbed his face. 'Okay, okay, okay. So let me get this straight. Farah just happens to show up at the Celsius Club. Like a fairy godmother. And she waves her magic wand and gives you some last-minute pixie dust. Late enough so that we fail to save Omar Badawi. But early enough so that we just about manage to capture Jamal Sidek…'

'Yeah.' Maya inhaled, her shoulders drawn tight. 'Yeah, that sums it up.'

'Uh-huh. Frankly, I don't know whether to laugh or to cry about this mindfuck.'

Kendra said, 'Well, Farah did give us a lucky break, even if it did force us to flex our original op.'

Adam said, 'You sound pretty perky for someone who came within a hair's breadth of getting your head blown off.'

'But I didn't. For which I'm grateful.'

'Righty-o.' Adam curled his lip. 'Look, I can't really make any sense of what Farah was trying to achieve…'

'Does it actually matter?' Kendra scoffed and pointed at Jamal on the gurney. 'Fact is, we got him. We *finally* got the bastard who killed Nathan. I'd say it's a freaking miracle. Pop the champagne. Sprinkle the confetti…'

'Oh yeah.' Adam slapped his palms together, rubbing them, his tone almost gleeful. 'We've got a few hours to spare. So I say we inflict as much pain on him as humanly possible. Then we liquidate his sorry ass. Make him disappear—'

Maya shook her head adamantly. 'No.'

Adam raised his eyebrows. *'No?'*

'No. We are not going to go down that road.'

Adam hesitated, then clicked his tongue, annoyed. 'Lest you forget, we're on a timer here, Maya. It won't be long before the CIA knuckle-draggers come crashing down on this party. And they're going to take Jamal away from us. You know they are.'

Kendra shrugged. 'You know, I hate to say it, but Adam has a point. Jamal is more valuable alive than dead to the CIA. They will want to squeeze him for intel. Which I suppose is fair enough. He's one of the most prominent *jihadi* field operatives in the war right now.'

Maya groaned, her hands resting on her hips, and she began to pace around in a semi-circle. 'Be that as it may, we're not going to spend what precious little time that we have torturing the man to death just because we feel like it.'

Adam said, 'Oh, for crying out loud. He murdered your father, Maya. Think of all the grief and devastation he inflicted on you and your mother. And think of how many other lives he's destroyed. This is the Butcher of Kajang we're talking about.'

'I know. I'm under no illusions about who he is.'

'So…?'

'So… I want to hear what he has to say first. From the horse's mouth.'

Adam grimaced. He looked like he was on the verge of saying something snarky. But then he paused, thinking better of it. And he shook his head and folded his arms. 'Okay. All right. We interrogate him. We sweat him out. But I don't know how much we're going to be able to get out of him within the time horizon that we've got.'

'If it comes down to it, we'll smuggle him out of the Blue Zone.'

'Hide out in the badlands?'

'Exactly.'

'And then what?'

'I haven't really figured out that part yet.'

'Oh jeez…'

Kendra glanced at Adam, then at Maya. She licked her lips and raised her hands in a placating gesture. 'It's your call, Maya. We'll back you either way.'

That's when Joel slipped off the surgical gloves he was wearing and gave a whistle as he stepped back from Jamal's gurney. 'We're done here. The patient is stable.'

Maya nodded. 'Outstanding. Let's get him set up…'

40

They wheeled Jamal into a specially prepared room, where the ceiling and walls had been lined with acoustic foam padding.

This was their makeshift interrogation centre, designed to muffle all noise.

Grim but necessary.

It was intended for Omar Badawi, but given the situation, it would work just as well for Jamal Sidek.

Vince and Joel positioned Jamal at the centre of the room and swivelled the gurney's hinges so that he was in a sitting position. Meanwhile, Kendra and Adam adjusted the halogen floor lights so that they were aimed directly at Jamal's face.

Vince looked at Maya. 'Ready?'

'Do it.'

Joel placed smelling salts under Jamal's nose, giving him a whiff. And Jamal immediately jerked awake, gasping, confused. He struggled against his restraints, and he winced from the bright lights, his eyes blinking furiously before narrowing into slits.

Maya spoke in Malay, 'Are you feeling sore? That's because we treated you and stitched up your wound. But we didn't give you any painkillers…'

Tensing his jaw, the cords of his neck straining, Jamal turned to look at Maya. But the leather strap on his forehead squeaked and held him in place, limiting his range of motion. He only managed a pitiful inch.

This annoyance was intentional. And just to make it that much harder on him, Maya positioned herself on the edge of his vision, forcing him to work for the simple act of turning his head to regard her. And even then, the harsh glare stabbed his eyes, causing him to squint, and all he would be able to see was her silhouette. He wouldn't be able to make out her features, nor her expression. All he had to go on was her voice.

This was Maya's way of exerting dominance over him.

Because she understood his psychological archetype all too well.

Jamal was a sniper — the kind of man who was used to calculating range and trajectory and windage. He strove for perfection. Mastering his mind and body for the sole purpose of putting steel on target.

It was all about discipline.

Focus.

Control.

How did you break a man like that?

Well, not with outright abuse and violence. Because that approach would be too obvious, and he was conditioned to resist and deflect that kind of pressure.

This was how a sniper like him could lie camouflaged at a hide site for hours and hours, controlling his breathing and heart rate, ignoring any distraction or discomfort, waiting for just the right moment to squeeze the trigger. Put steel on target.

So, if you really wanted to get under his skin, you had to introduce an itch on the subconscious level. An itch that was ever-present. One that he couldn't readily scratch for relief. And then you had to amplify it, make it even more insistent.

And slowly, surely, you would disrupt his finely tuned sense of equilibrium. Chip away at his mental pillars of support. Weaken him from within.

Problem was, Maya knew that they didn't have the benefit of time. So she had to accelerate her interrogation programme. Outline the stakes as quickly as possible.

Maya said, 'The Shiites want you. The Americans want you. And, I'm just guessing, the Sunni Wahhabis have a problem with you as well. That other man you were fighting up on that office building — he was supposed to be your spotter, wasn't he? But, for some reason, he turned on you. Or… did you turn on him?'

Jamal was silent, but from his trembling cheeks, Maya knew that she had hit a raw nerve.

She pushed on. 'Omar Badawi was a coordinator. He provided you with safe houses. He sheltered you from the Shiites and the Americans. And yet you killed him. Tell me, are you in the habit of betraying all your friends?'

This was a question designed to challenge Jamal's sense of honour.

Betraying a benefactor was a big taboo in Malay culture.

It was considered shameful.

Jamal managed a defiant smile, his voice weak. 'Your *Bahasa Melayu* is good. You speak the language almost like a local. But not quite. You have a very mild accent.'

Maya shook her head ever so slightly. She could see what he was trying to do. He was trying to turn the conversation around and switch the focus to her. To gain reprieve from his own mounting anxiety. But, no, she wasn't going to let him off that easy.

Maya said, 'You're the son of an *uztaz*, but you didn't want to follow in your father's religious footsteps. So, in an act of youthful rebellion, you gained a scholarship and attended Royal Military College. Malaysia's version of Sandhurst. You graduated number three in your class. Then you entered the Navy. Qualified for PASKAL special forces. Saw action in Borneo and the Gulf of Aden. Highly decorated. And then you suddenly gave it all up. Resigned your commission as an officer. And you went over to join the Wahhabi militia in what you call the Great Cleansing. Your record goes black after that. Lots of speculation. Lots of rumour…'

Maya paused for dramatic effect.

She continued, her tone mocking now, 'Forgive me, but I find it really surprising. How a man like you rejects a religious upbringing, goes into the secular military, then suddenly changes direction. Swings back to the path of religion. It's almost as if… well, you could not escape your father's shadow.'

Jamal's smile dipped. 'Do not talk about my father. You know nothing about him.'

'I know he was a man of peace. And, if he were alive today, he'd probably be disappointed in you…'

'Stop it—'

'Imagine how things would have been if you'd never stepped outside the straight and narrow path in the first place.'

'No, stop—'

Maya went for the jugular now. 'Imagine how things would be for your family now.'

That was it.

That was the itch.

Jamal swallowed, his posture stiffening. 'Somehow I always knew that this day would come. My life is forfeit. But my family need not pay for my sins. They *must not* pay for my sins.'

Maya nodded slowly. 'The *caliphate* is holding your family?'

'Yes…' Jamal dropped his gaze, his sweaty face pulled tight in anguish. 'Yes. They keep my family hidden in a safe house in Kajang so long as I continue to serve. But…'

'But…?'

'But I am no longer a believer in their cause. This was why I fought with my spotter. He threatened my family because I refused to kill civilians.' Jamal hesitated. 'Omar Badawi was fair game because he indulged in *haram* activities. But I could not bring myself to hurt civilians. That was one line I could not cross.'

Maya considered it.

Badawi was deader than dead. So were his bodyguards. And, yeah, a few bouncers were down for the count as well. But, so far as Maya knew, no patrons were killed at the Celsius Club.

Jamal's story seemed to hold up. He wasn't a zealot. He wasn't a fanatic. Just a professional out to do an op. Until the op interfered with his conscience.

Jamal lifted his gaze, his eyes crinkling. He spoke in English now, 'I want to make a deal.'

Maya played along, switching to English as well. 'And what makes you think we'd be willing to consider one?'

'When we met in that office, you looked familiar. So familiar. But I could not remember where I had seen you before. But… now I know. Now it is clear to me.' Jamal paused, his voice falling to a hoarse whisper. 'You are Maya Raines, daughter of Nathan Raines…'

Maya inhaled, her throat feeling like fish hooks. Just hearing him say her father's name was enough to provoke her ire. And she wanted nothing more than to lunge at him and strangle him.

It would be so easy.

Oh so easy.

Christ…

It took everything she had not to give into that desire.

Maya shook, her face feeling hot, her hands fidgeting by her sides. 'If you know who I am, then you know that I hate you. I hate you with a passion. And now that I have you, I absolutely intend to make you pay for what you've done…'

'I regret my actions,' Jamal said. 'I was foolish in those days. I was deluded about what the Great Cleansing would bring—'

Maya growled. 'Nathan Raines wanted to stop the war from happening. He was a Westerner, sure, but he loved this country. He wanted to stop it from descending into chaos. And by killing him — *by murdering him* — you derailed his good intentions.'

'I am sorry.'

'Sorry isn't good enough. Sorry doesn't make things right.'

That's when Maya felt a hand resting on her shoulder, squeezing. It was Adam, expressing his concern. But Maya just shrugged him off.

She could handle this.

She *had* to handle this.

This was her cross to bear.

Jamal spoke, his tone pleading now, 'My life is well and truly forfeit. But I know you are an honourable woman.' His eyes welled up with tears. 'Help my family, and I shall give you everything I know. Weapon caches, safe houses, supply routes, troop movements. *Everything.*'

Maya just stared at Jamal, wrestling with her own emotions, her mouth twitching.

She tried to make up her mind about what to do next.

That's when Kendra leaned in close and whispered in Maya's ear, 'Let's talk about this outside.'

41

They left Jamal and stepped outside the interrogation room.

Kendra shut the door. 'You know, I think there's something we can work with here.'

Adam was incredulous, and he gave a cynical snort. 'I can't believe you're even considering this horseshit. For all we know, it could be a major set-up. He could be leading us into a trap.'

Maya sighed. 'I studied his microexpressions. I don't think he's lying.'

'I'm sorry, but you're not being objective. He's pulling your heartstrings with all this talk about his family, and he's doing it on purpose—'

That's when Joel's laptop at the workbench interrupted them with a chiming sound. Joel hurried over to it. 'We've finished decrypting all the data we intercepted from Omar Badawi's phone.'

Kendra nodded. 'Okay. And…?'

Joel hunched over the computer, scrolling through the files eagerly. 'And… what I'm seeing are architectural floor plans. Looks like a safe house in Kajang. It matches up to what Jamal mentioned.'

'Mm-hm.' Kendra snapped her fingers. 'Well, folks, there you go. It's real. It's actionable.'

'*Good God.*' Adam raised both his hands and rubbed the back of his head in frustration. 'Are you seriously suggesting that we infiltrate Kajang to perform a rescue mission? *Really?*'

'Yeah, really.'

'Why in the hell should we be risking ourselves for this *jihadi* murderer? He doesn't deserve our help.'

Maya groaned. 'It's not about him. It's about his family. Can't you see? This right here is our chance to do something good. Something decent. And if this intel pans out…' Maya turned and pointed at the floor plans on Joel's laptop. 'Isn't it justification enough? Isn't this what Papa — the great and legendary Nathan Raines — would have wanted us to pursue? To do something… righteous?'

No one spoke.

The silence stretched.

A feeling of poignancy hung heavy in the air between them.

Eventually Kendra said, 'Agreed. It's what Nathan would have wanted. He always put innocent lives first…'

Adam grumbled under his breath, 'Right. Fine. Let's take a pleasant stroll out to Kajang, kick some ass and save Jamal's family. And then what? What do we do with them afterwards?'

Vince exchanged a look with Joel, and they traded words in rapid-fire Hebrew.

Adam stared at them, irritated. 'If you have something to say, say it in English.'

Joel nodded cautiously. 'We may have a suggestion.'

'Well, spit it out, then.'

Vince said, 'We have the necessary *sayanim* contacts. Once we secure Jamal's family, we can find a way to extract them all to Singapore. And from there, we can offer them asylum in Israel.'

Maya arched her eyebrows. 'What's the catch?'

'Jamal will become an asset for us. He gives us what he promised. Weapon caches, safe houses, supply routes, troop movements. *Everything.*'

Maya considered the proposal. 'Can you guarantee that Jamal and his family will have new cover identities?'

Joel said, 'We can.'

'Close protection?'

'Yes.'

'Comfortable housing? Good schooling?'

'That is what we intend to provide.'

Maya took a breath and exhaled. 'Okay, then. Let's make it happen.'

'Ooh, nice one.' Kendra chuckled and slapped Vince and Joel on their backs. 'And they say that Metsada operators don't have warm and fuzzy hearts.'

Vince smirked. 'We do not have warm and fuzzy hearts. This is just a cold political calculation on our part.'

'Yeah, whatever. Keep up the tough-guy act. You're not fooling anyone.'

Maya opened the door, and they stepped back into the interrogation room.

Vince and Joel unbuckled Jamal from his restraints, and they fed him ibuprofen pills for pain relief. Then they briefed him on what their extraction plan was going to be.

Jamal listened quietly and accepted the proposal without question, then pressed his hand against his heart. It was a traditional Malay gesture of appreciation. 'Thank you. Thank you so much for believing in me.'

Maya said, 'This doesn't change anything between us. I'm only doing this for your family. Despite everything, I don't think they deserve to be deprived of a husband and a father.'

Jamal blinked, and he bowed his head, his face brimming with emotion. 'I understand. You still have my gratitude nonetheless.'

Adam glared at Jamal. 'You better not be lying to us. Otherwise…' Adam performed a throat-slashing gesture, making an ominous hissing sound as he did.

Kendra sighed in disapproval and nudged Adam with her elbow. 'Let's just reserve judgement on the poor man until we get a chance to see the area of operations for ourselves.'

'Okay.' Maya nodded. 'Let's get everything packed up, shall we? We leave in fifteen mikes.'

42

Getting out of the Blue Zone didn't come cheap.

Maya had to pay a Malaysian army captain named Syed an initial bribe of one-hundred-thousand American dollars before he agreed to give them safe passage through the checkpoints. She told him that they were private contractors out to conduct a reconnaissance mission, and Syed seemed to buy it.

It was pretty much shaking hands with the devil, but for lack of a better option, it would have to do.

Bringing Jamal along, Maya and her team climbed into an MRAP All-Terrain Vehicle. It was a rolling monstrosity of reinforced steel, riding high on six armoured wheels, designed to defend against bomb attacks.

The crew compartment was cramped, smelling of sweat and grease and gunpowder, and when the MRAP moved, its turbocharged diesel engine roared. To Maya, it felt a lot like being sealed up inside an iron coffin, with only tiny ballistic windows to look out of. This certainly wasn't for the claustrophobic or faint of heart.

As part of a small convoy of armoured vehicles, they departed through one of the southern corridors, bypassing all the sectors patrolled by American troops. The relationship between Putrajaya and Washington was at an all-time low, which meant that the coordination between the two sides was minimal.

They cleared the Blue Zone with no trouble at all, and Captain Syed and his platoon hit the highway, steering straight into the heart of *jihadi* territory.

They experienced no harassment. No ambushes. No delays.

The journey was smooth as silk.

And why not?

It was no secret that the Malaysian military and the Wahhabi extremists had a tacit agreement when it came to their conduct on the battlefield. They had a common enemy — the Shiite insurgents. Which meant that the Malaysian military did what they could to protect key government interests, but otherwise, they left the Wahhabis to roam free and commit atrocities against the Shiites. And, in return, the Wahhabis avoided targeting Malaysian soldiers.

It was a sweetheart deal that allowed the civil war to perpetuate itself many times over.

Ordinarily, Maya would have been outraged by the duplicity of it all.

But, in this instance, it worked to Maya's advantage.

It was the only way to slip into Kajang in the dead of night without getting shot up or blown up in the process. And, at the end of it all, if they managed to complete their mission and get out in one piece, Maya had promised Syed another two-hundred-thousand dollars. Greed was a good motivator, and Maya hoped that it was enough for him to keep his mouth shut and look the other way.

Of course, there were no guarantees that he wouldn't just betray them to the *jihadis*.

But, under the circumstances, this was a risk worth taking.

Their chances were roughly fifty-fifty.

Right now, Maya was strapped into a bucket seat, feet braced against the reinforced steel floor, swaying with the vehicle's movement. And Jamal was beside her, their shoulders almost touching.

Maya had a tablet on her lap, and she was studying the safe-house floor plans, as well as screenshots of the property and the neighbourhood taken from Google Earth.

It wasn't high-resolution.

It wasn't real-time.

Certainly nothing like what the CIA could provide her in terms of actual surveillance overflights.

Maya wasn't exactly thrilled with the idea of improvising like this. But she would have to settle for what she could get.

Maya gave Jamal a sidelong glance. 'What kind of opposing force are we up against?'

'There will be ten men guarding the bungalow. Four of them will be patrolling the compound's perimeter at all times.'

'How good are they?'

'They have some combat experience. But nothing extensive.'

'So… they're basically Tier Two militants.'

'It would be more accurate to describe them as Tier Three.'

'Right. That's reassuring. Now, how do we get into the property? What's the best point of ingress?'

Jamal pointed at the screen. 'You see that big *longkang* just south-east of the house?'

Maya squinted. And, yes, she saw it. There was a gully with a storm-water drain visible. It snaked all the way to the rear of the compound wall.

Jamal said, 'By using this line of approach, we should be able to evade the patrols and close in on our objective.'

'Okay. And once we penetrate the target building, your family will be on the top floor?'

'Yes, for safety, my wife, son and daughter will all sleep in the same room.'

'I'm assuming it's the master bedroom?'

'Correct.'

'You're certain?'

'Yes, those were my instructions to my family. And they will always abide by my instructions.'

'Good to know.' Maya inhaled and nodded. 'All right. Now, given all the drama that happened in Bukit Bintang earlier, is there any chance at all that news might filter back to the *jihadis*? Will they increase their level of readiness?'

'They will only know what they hear on the radio or see on television. Beyond that, Mustapha and I are not meant to check in for the next twenty-four hours. I do not believe they will suspect anything.'

'You sound like you're guessing.'

Jamal tilted his head and puckered his lips. 'Yes. Yes, I am guessing.'

'Okay. Here's my big question: once we move in and engage them, will the sentries fall back to protect your family, or will they do something else? What's their standard operating procedure?'

Jamal shook his head, his expression pained. 'I cannot say for sure. It's clear to me now that Mustapha was not the comrade I thought he was.'

'What does that mean?'

'That means that he informed on me to the *Emir*. And he could have left instructions with these men to… liquidate my family if the situation becomes troublesome.'

Maya frowned. 'Could he really be that spiteful?'

Jamal gave a throaty chuckle. 'For a *mujahid* like me to lose my faith and abandon the cause is seen as the greatest act of betrayal. The *caliphate* has no tolerance and no mercy. You have no idea what they are capable of doing…'

Maya thought back to the dead people that she'd seen strung up on lamp posts, the memory of it making her stomach turn. 'Actually, I do have some idea. I've seen first-hand how the Wahhabis punish their enemies in Rawang.'

'Then you understand what is at stake. If my family are lucky, they will die swiftly. But if they are not so lucky...' Jamal trailed off, allowing the implied threat to stand.

Maya scowled, narrowing her eyes. 'We'll do all we can to make sure it doesn't come to that. You have my word.'

43

Kajang was deep in the heart of Sunni territory in the badlands.

As hostile as you could get.

Fortunately, the Malaysian army maintained a small garrison in a forward-operating base here. It wasn't anything fancy. Just an old Catholic church surrounded by razor wire, concrete barriers and machine-gun emplacements. A staging point for supply and refuelling.

That's where the convoy came to a stop, and Maya and her team dismounted from the MRAP. At the steps of the church, they did final checks on their weapons, ammunition and gear.

Above them, swollen clouds gathered, and thunder rumbled.

The air felt sticky and humid.

It was going to rain soon.

Captain Syed approached Maya. 'This is as far as we can take you. After this, you are on your own.'

Maya said, 'Understood. If we make it out of this alive, you will get the remaining two-hundred-thousand as part of our agreement.'

Syed adjusted his helmet and gave her a sceptical look. 'Forgive me for saying so, but you mercenaries are crazy for venturing into *jihadi* territory. If they find you, they will cut you into pieces.'

'Yes, well, let's hope for the best...'

'Be warned: we won't be able to save you if things go bad. We won't be acting as your quick-reaction force.'

'Believe me, I'm not expecting you to.' Maya gave him a dismissive smile. 'All you have to do is keep your mouth shut and stand down until we're in the clear. This will be the easiest two-hundred-thousand you will ever make.'

Syed scoffed and turned away, muttering under his breath, 'So be it. I wish you the best.'

Vince was helping Jamal slip on a bulletproof vest. 'I can never get used to the insolence of the local military.'

Joel attached a suppressor to the barrel of his HK416 rifle. 'And I can never get used to the extraordinary corruption they practise. It's insufferable.'

Maya shrugged and exchanged a knowing glance with Jamal. 'It looks like we're being forced to come to terms with a lot of things today, aren't we?'

Jamal tilted his head, his lips pulled tight. 'Indeed we are.'

Maya pulled a satellite phone out from the chest rig she wore over her body armour. She powered it on and dialled Chief Lucas Raynor.

The satphone had signal-scrambling features, which would mask her location. But she was fully aware that with enough time and effort, the CIA analysts could track her.

But Maya didn't intend to give them the opportunity to do so.

This would just be a short call.

For the sake of courtesy.

Maya pressed the phone to her ear, and there was a series of melodic tones as the encryption took hold and performed the necessary handshake.

Maya waited.

Eventually Raynor's voice came on the line, sounding tinny and hollow. 'Yes?'

'Sir, it's me.'

There was a sharp intake of air. 'Maya? *Goddamn it.* You are going to tell me exactly where you are and what the hell you're doing.'

Maya cleared her throat. 'I'm in the badlands at the moment.'

'*What?* In the badlands? Where exactly?'

'Can't tell you. I'm right in the middle of a sensitive op at the moment.'

'Maya, you've gone way off reservation here. You need to cease and desist—'

'I'm sorry, sir. I will update you as soon as I can. Promise.'

And with that, Maya disconnected the call, killed the phone's power and removed the battery.

Adam was watching. He smirked and thumbed his nose. 'Let me guess. He wanted to nominate you for the Distinguished Intelligence Medal for your outstanding service.'

Maya sighed. She rubbed her face, then smoothed her hair. 'Nope. Definitely not.'

Kendra said, 'Well, look on the bright side, eh? At least the chief can't say we didn't check in with him.'

'Yeah, for all the good that's gonna do.'

44

They set off from the base in electric scooters, riding in twos.

Adam and Maya.
Kendra and Joel.
Vince and Jamal.

The scooters didn't have really good acceleration or a great maximum top speed. But that wasn't the point. The point was to maintain a low profile.

Their engines were close to silent, and they rode with their lights off, relying on night-vision goggles only.

At three in the morning, the streets were almost deserted. Like most districts in the badlands, the power grid here was unreliable. The street lamps were non-functional. That gave them large tracts of darkness to conceal their advance.

Joel launched a small tri-rotor drone and used it to scout the route ahead of them. It gave him a bird's-eye video feed, helping him identify *jihadi* roadblocks and patrols. He guided the team around those obstacles, vectoring in on the bungalow where Jamal's family was being held.

They covered the five-kilometre distance with no trouble at all.

45

They parked their scooters at the foot of the hill overlooking the bungalow, hiding the vehicles with camouflaged netting. Then they crawled up the slope, hugging the ground, using the tall grass and thorny shrubs as cover.

That's when the swollen clouds finally broke. It started to rain, a loose pitter-patter at first, but the deluge grew heavier, soaking the soil, turning it muddy.

That made the climb more arduous. Maya was drenched. Her clothes were slimy. Her skin prickled from the wind.

But, all in all, she considered this development a good one.

The rough weather would provide them with additional concealment.

Soon enough they reached the summit of the hill.

Taking cover behind a rocky outcrop, Joel set up an RF jammer on the ground. It looked like a small satellite dish, and its purpose was to disrupt all radio and cell signals in the area by throwing up a blanket of white noise. Anyone trying to make or receive a call would only get static.

The team's own communication network, of course, would remain functional. They were operating on an encrypted bandwidth, which was exempt from the effects of the jammer.

Vince used the drone to do several discrete flyovers over the compound below, while the rest of the team gathered around him and peered at his tablet computer. Unlike regular devices, this one had a screen that used a red filter. It restricted the glare and kept it localised, and no one beyond their immediate vicinity would be able to spot it.

Adam gave a low whistle. 'Fancy looking place they set your family up in, Jamal. You ought to be proud.'

Jamal gave a grim nod. 'This is nothing more but a fancy prison.'

Maya studied the video feed.

The compound was ringed by high walls covered in vines, and the estate was shaded by fruit trees. Two teams of *jihadi* sentries orbited the perimeter, flashlights gleaming.

The house itself was old and grand, dating back to the British colonial era. Two storeys. Most of the windows were dark, but some were bright, with *jihadis* occasionally visible behind the curtains and blinds. And at the rear of the property, there was a large diesel generator operating, which accounted for the electricity.

Maya really wished they could get penetrating thermal scans of the house. So they could get an accurate fix on the positions of all the hostiles inside. But, no, that just wasn't possible. Not with the simple tri-rotor drone they had. For now, all they had to go on was educated guesswork.

Maya wiped rainwater from her face. 'All right. This is how it's going to work. Kendra here will be pulling sniper duty. She'll give us an overwatch. The rest of us will infiltrate the target building. Slow and steady does it.'

Jamal fidgeted anxiously. 'I will need a weapon.'

Maya stared at him. 'Negative. I don't trust you enough to give you one.'

'But—'

'No buts. What I will allow you to do, though, is act as our cargo mule.'

'Cargo... *what?*'

'Mule. You can carry breaching charges and M72 launchers for us. In the event things get hot and loud, we might need them.'

Jamal wrinkled up his nose in disgust, looking like he wanted to argue some more. But after a moment of consternation, he sighed, shaking his head. 'As you wish. But this is what I used to tell my men when I served in the navy — once you pull the trigger, you cannot take back your bullet. So, please, I beg you to watch your gunfire.'

Kendra offered a sympathetic smile as she started unfolding the bipod on her Arctic Warfare sniper rifle. 'Of course. We will watch our background. Clean shots only.'

'My family's safety is in your hands.'

'We won't let you down.'

Adam sucked on his teeth impatiently. 'Yeah, yeah. Enough with the hand-holding and the Kumbaya. Let's rock and roll, shall we?'

46

With Kendra covering them, they stacked up and formed a tactical train.

Adam was in the front, acting as the point man.

Maya occupied the second position.

Jamal was third.

Vince was fourth.

And Joel was last in the stack, acting as the rearguard.

'Stand by to stand by,' Maya whispered.

She waited in anticipation until the *jihadi* patrol closest to their intended route had made a pass and swung away to the opposite direction.

'Go, go, go,' Maya said.

They rose as one, and moving in a single file, they descended the side of the hill, their boots squelching, the rain pelting against them.

With their HK416 rifles at the high-ready, they powered forward in a steady clip. They reached the gully ahead, and they dropped into the storm drain, sliding down the concrete culvert, fast-flowing water splashing beneath them.

They started going against the current, advancing towards the compound.

They only managed fifty metres when Kendra's voice came over the net. 'All elements. Hold, hold, hold. You have two tangos almost upon you. I repeat, two tangos. Danger close…'

Adam raised his fist, and the entire team caterpillared to a halt.

They crouched and flattened themselves against the side of the drain.

Through her night-vision goggles, Maya could just about make out the individual beams of two flashlights puncturing the darkness above them, swaying back and forth.

Voices drifted.

Footsteps approached.

Closer…

Closer…

Maya kept one hand on her gun, gripping it at the low-ready. With her other hand, she signalled her team discretely, telling them to hold fast.

'I have a solution,' Kendra said. 'Going weapons-free in five… four… three… two… one…'

There were two hollow thumps, barely discernible amidst the wind and thunder. The echo of Kendra firing her suppressed rifle. Then came the sound of bodies tumbling against the soil above.

Kendra said, 'X-rays neutralised.'

Immediately, Vince and Joel sprung into action, climbing over the lip of the embankment, and they grabbed the dead *jihadis* by their legs, pulling them down into the drain, hiding them from sight.

At the same time, Adam collected their Kalashnikov rifles, as well as their flashlights, switching them off.

Jamal stared at the *jihadis* lying splayed out in the water beside him, their skulls cracked open like broken eggshells, leaking blood. 'I knew this man.' Jamal pointed at the *jihadi* closest to him, the edges of his mouth twitching, his voice strained. 'His name was Ismail. We used to serve together…'

Maya said nothing. She just waited, allowing Jamal a moment to come to terms with it.

Adam, though, was less patient. He was disassembling the Kalashnikovs into individual pieces, tossing them in separate directions. 'Well, fuck it. Ismail here was on the wrong side of history. Nothing to get sentimental about.'

'Of course.' Jamal swallowed and regained his composure. 'Of course.'

Maya said, 'Moving.'

Kendra said, 'Covering.'

The team continued pushing forward once more, until they reached the end of the drain. Then they climbed out and cautiously flip-flopped towards the compound wall, taking turns covering one another until they were all in position.

That's when Kendra spoke, 'Scalpel Two for Scalpel One. Hold, hold, hold. A tango just came out on to the main balcony. He's smoking a cigarette and gazing out.'

Maya whispered into her throat mic, 'Say again? Main balcony?'

'Affirmative. Main balcony.' Kendra paused. 'I have a solution.'

Maya knew what that meant. Kendra had the sentry in her crosshairs, and if need be, she could remove him from the equation.

Problem was, dropping him now would still make a noise, no matter how minor. And given his close proximity to the master bedroom, there was every chance that a member of Jamal's family could hear it and react. Or — *God forbid* — another sentry could get nosy and investigate.

Could they risk it?

Maya shook her head. Now that they were so close to their objective, stealth was essential. There was no sense in engaging the enemy prematurely. Not until they were in complete control of the battlespace.

Maya said, 'Negative on contact. Let's wait him out.'

Kendra said, 'Copy. Standing down.'

The seconds ticked by.

Maya looked at Jamal.

He nodded ever so slightly and silently mouthed his thanks, appreciating Maya for not putting his family in undue danger.

Kendra said, 'Okay, tango's finished his smoko break. He's stepping back inside. You're clear to move, but you should double-time it.'

'Roger. Moving now.'

Adam boosted Maya over the wall first.

Then Jamal was next.

Then Vince.

Then Joel.

Then, with a running start, Adam leapt — and Vince and Joel were waiting to catch him by his outstretched arms, yanking him up and over the wall.

They were all safely inside the compound now.

Adam led the team towards the nearest cluster of fruit trees, and they crouched there amidst the soggy leaves and swaying branches, taking in their surroundings, weapons scanning for threats.

With low whispers, they acknowledged their sectors of fire.

'Back clear.'

'Left clear.'

'Right clear.'

'All clear.'

Maya said, 'Moving.'

Kendra said, 'Covering.'

They leapfrogged forward and stacked up at the rear of the house. The chugging of the diesel generator, along with the rain drumming against the house, provided ambient noise to cover their infiltration.

Vince slapped an EMP charge on the side of the generator and armed it. The advantage of using an electromagnetic pulse here was that it would be near-silent. Much better than using a plastic explosive.

Adam crept up a flight of cement steps, moved across a raised patio, then knelt beside the kitchen door. He got out a fibrescope. He snaked the lens under the door and peered through the eyepiece, checking for tripwires or sensors.

Finding none, he worked on the door with a lockpick.

He gave a thumbs-up when he got it open—

That's when Maya heard something new. It was the telltale roar of car engines approaching in the distance. She frowned and cocked her head.

Kendra said, 'Scalpel Two for Scalpel One. We have incoming. I see three vehicles entering the neighbourhood from the north. Two technicals and one regular pickup truck. I count… twelve hostiles. I say again, twelve hostiles…'

47

Maya couldn't help but flinch, her mouth going dry.
Shit...
She immediately assumed the worst. Their op had been blown, and reinforcements were coming.
Not good. Not good at all...
Maya whispered, 'What's their vector and ETA?'
'Hold one,' Kendra said.
Maya waited with her breath caught in her throat.
The moment stretched, unbearably tense.
Kendra said, 'Okay, vehicles have peeled off now and taken a side street. They are stopping at one of the other bungalows. North-west. Approximately three-hundred metres from you. Their postures look relaxed. Feels like a bed-down site.'
Maya exhaled, relieved.
So... these new X-rays weren't actually here for them. They were part of a separate force stationed close by. A coincidence.
Which meant that, right now, they had three separate threats to worry about.
Firstly — the six *jihadis* present within the house itself.
Secondly — the two *jihadis* still out on foot patrol.
Thirdly — the twelve *jihadis* positioned downrange.
It was manageable.
And Maya figured it was time to thin the herd a little. 'Do you have eyes on the two tangos still out on the perimeter?'

Kendra said, 'Copy that. They're just east of me. I have a solution.'

'Scorpio.'

Maya heard two thumps in her earpiece.

Kendra said, 'Done. And… done. Tangos neutralised. Two for the price of one.'

'Much appreciated. Thank you.'

48

Adam was first through the kitchen door, and the rest of them followed, flowing through the breach, fanning out, guns at the high-ready. They dripped water on the tiled floor, their soft-soled boots squeaking ever so slightly.

The kitchen was dark and empty, with only the sound of the refrigerator humming in the corner. They moved past the stoves, past the pantry, and they slipped into the corridor beyond.

This was a fatal funnel, where if a hostile chanced upon them and fired wildly, they would all be cut to pieces.

So they could not afford to linger.

They advanced quickly, staying as close to the walls as possible without actually brushing against them in order to minimise noise.

They cleared other dark rooms along their path.

The dining room.

The study room.

The laundry room.

The drawing room.

Just around the corner ahead was the living room, and Maya saw light spilling out into the hallway, accompanied by the melodious tempo of Islamic *nashid* music.

Maya flipped up her night-vision goggles, and with Adam covering her, she got out a fibrescope, and she angled it to peer around the corner.

She counted three tangos in the living room, watching the television. Two were seated on the sofa; one was seated in an armchair. Their Kalashnikov rifles were propped up against the tea table beside them, just barely out of reach.

There were still three *jihadis* left unaccounted for.

Probably upstairs.

But, yeah, for now, Maya would settle for what she could get.

She put away her fibrescope and eased her night-vision goggles back down. She gestured at her team, signalling them to get ready to go tactical, and she performed a countdown with her fingers.

Five...

Four...

Three...

Two...

One...

Execute...

Vince tapped a button on his watch and set off the EMP charge, and the generator at the rear of the house was disabled.

The lights fizzled out.

The television went silent.

The *jihadis* were caught by surprise.

That's when the team surged into the living room.

Adam and Maya drifted left.

Vince and Joel drifted right.

They took up points of domination in the room, their infrared lasers glittering, locking on to their targets.

Then they let rip, suppressed gunshots chattering.

The tangos didn't stand a chance.

Two of them died where they sat, their bodies jerking from the bullet impacts, the stuffing from the sofa cushions exploding and misting the air.

The third *jihadi* just about managed to rise from his armchair, fumbling for his Kalashnikov rifle. But it didn't do him much good. His head erupted, and he lurched back, the chair toppling as he went down hard.

Maya and her team stopped shooting.

The brass shells from their weapons tinkled hollowly on the floor.

The room smelled of hot metal and gunsmoke.

With urgent whispers, they each acknowledged their sectors of fire.

'Clear front.'

'Clear left.'

'Clear right.'

'All clear.'

49

They exited the living room and reached the staircase in the foyer.

They stacked up and climbed.

The wooden steps were old and creaky, sounding unbearably loud under their weight. The noise grated on Maya. But — *damn it* — there was no way to disguise their ascent, no matter how carefully they moved.

They cleared the first flight of steps, reaching the landing beyond. They button-hooked around the U-shaped corner, and they began creeping up the next flight of steps.

They were about halfway up when a shadow suddenly appeared at the top of the staircase, toting a flashlight. He spoke in Malay, irritated. 'Samsul, is that you? Did you trip the power again?'

Adam fired two rounds into the tango's face, and he toppled back, his flashlight spinning.

That's when another voice came from further away. 'Hussein? *Hussein?* What is going on out there?'

Maya craned her neck, and she caught a flicker of movement — a *jihadi* leaning out from behind a hallway, Kalashnikov rifle held at the ready, his eyes widening.

Maya snapped off three rounds at him, but he just about managed to reel back, and her bullets walloped against the wall where his head had been. A close miss.

The tango screamed, 'Intruders! *Intruders!*' And keeping himself hidden behind the corner, he twisted his rifle around, opening up on full automatic, firing blind.

The ear-splitting barrage was absolutely volcanic within the confines of the house.

Bullets hissed and cracked, slashing the banister on the staircase, wood splintering.

Adam was forced to duck, and Maya did the same, hurling herself against the steps.

Behind them, from the landing below, Vince and Joel returned fire in sustained bursts, blowing apart chunks of the wall where the *jihadi* was hiding behind, forcing him to retreat further back into the hallway.

The brief lull in the gunfight gave Adam, Maya and Jamal an opportunity to scramble to the top of the stairs, and they lunged and positioned themselves beside the hallway.

That's when the shooting started again, but it was fiercer this time.

Maya could hear two Kalashnikov rifles roaring in unison, and right in front of her, a window frame exploded, glass fragments shrieking, tattered curtains billowing.

A second tango had clearly joined in the fight.

Jamal was distraught. 'My family is in the bedroom at the end of that corridor.'

Maya nodded. 'I know. I remember the floor plan.'

'We need to reach them.'

'We will.'

Maya signalled Vince and Joel to move forward and provide covering fire, keeping the tangos occupied. Then Maya and Adam drew stun grenades, pulled their pins, and tossed them around the corner.

'Flash out,' Maya said.

The grenades bounced down the corridor and exploded in a blaze of dazzling light.

The hostile gunfire immediately ceased.

The *jihadis* were gasping and cursing.

That's when Maya and Adam swung into the hallway.

Maya aimed high.

Adam aimed low.

They sliced past the bend in the corridor, and Maya came across one *jihadi* stumbling about, hunched over, clawing at his face, blinded and deafened by the explosion.

There was no hesitation; no mercy.

At point-blank range, Maya and Adam riddled him with double taps, and he went down.

Maya vaulted over the body, hitting the next corner, searching for the other *jihadi*—

That's when she heard the sound of hobbling footsteps and a door swinging on its hinges and slamming shut just ahead of her.

The tango had retreated into the master bedroom.

Damn it…

That seriously complicated matters.

All the *jihadi* had to do was cover the only point of ingress — the doorway — and if they tried to made entry, he would just cut them down as they came through. It was the perfect definition of a fatal funnel.

But Maya and her team had come prepared for this eventuality.

They would bypass the door entirely.

Jamal unslung his backpack, and he passed out breaching charges. His eyes were desperate. 'My family is in there. Be careful, please.'

Maya nodded. 'We will be.'

Working quickly, Adam, Vince and Joel attached the explosives to separate sections of the bedroom wall. These weren't regular charges. They were filled with water bladders, which would keep the blast radius localised and produce minimal fragmentation.

It was safe for the team.

It was safe for Jamal's family in the room within.

Adam strung all the charges together to a single detonator. He called out, 'Fire in the hole. Three, two, one.'

Adam hit the trigger.

Boom. Boom. Boom...

Simultaneous blasts rippled across the wall, and the sections cratered inward, brick and plaster vaporising, creating horizontal holes which acted as gun ports for Vince and Joel to aim into the room.

Meanwhile, the third hole was larger and vertical, acting as an entry port for Maya. Compacting her body, she lunged through it just as Vince and Joel sighted down on the *jihadi*, snapping off single shots at him.

Joel yelled, 'Contact left. *Left.*'

Maya hit the floor in the bedroom beyond in a dive-roll.

She came up on one knee, sliding.

The *jihadi* was to her left, staggering forward, wounded in the stomach. He was gripping his Kalashnikov rifle one-handed, pivoting it around.

Through the swirling smoke and dust, Maya caught a glimpse of Puteri and Rania huddled on the bed, clinging on to each other, terrified.

The tango screamed, *'Allahu akbar!'*

The bastard was trying to kill Jamal's family.

Everything was unfolding in slow motion now.

Panting through her teeth, her heart hammering in her ears, Maya leaned into her weapon and planted her laser on the tango.

She fanned her trigger, shooting him twice, then twice more.

The *jihadi* convulsed and fell against a cabinet door, smashing through, blood staining the clothes in the wardrobe beyond. As he slumped to the floor, his face going slack, he somehow managed one last death squeeze on his rifle's trigger.

A final burst of gunfire erupted, raking across the ceiling, fragments raining down.

Then everything went quiet and still.

Maya relaxed her aim, exhaling. She turned to look at Jamal's wife and daughter. They were frightened but unharmed. Yes, she managed to save them. Just in time—

That's when Maya suddenly became aware of movement shuffling behind her. Another threat. Maya reacted, starting to turn, and that's when she felt someone body-slam her.

She hit the floor roughly, falling on top of her rifle, gashing her chin, her night-vision goggles going askew.

She felt the full weight of an assailant on top of her, pinning her down.

There was a swishing sound, and instinctively, Maya just about managed to shift her head to one side, and a knife hissed past, its point scraping against the floor.

Maya was confused.

Why wasn't anyone firing a shot to help her?

Shit...

Maya seized her opponent's wrist, trapping his arm, stopping him from using his knife any further, and then powering her hips, twisting hard, she managed to throw him off her back, the knife clattering, and she drew her pistol and swept it around, feeling the curve of her trigger—

That's when Jamal crashed through the bedroom door, leaping between Maya and her opponent, his palms outstretched, gesturing frantically. 'No, no! Don't do it!'

Blinking hard, Maya eased off her trigger.

She got a good look at her opponent for the first time.

It was Jamal's son.

Imran...

The boy rose and took a shaky step forward, his face knotted in disbelief. 'Is that you, Father? Is that really you?'

Jamal turned and embraced his son, tousling his hair. 'Indeed. It's me, my son. I'm here.'

'I... I tried to be a warrior, Father. I tried to protect our family.'

'I know. Your heart is pure.'

Puteri approached, carrying Rania in her arms. And the entire family came together in a massive bear hug, laughing and crying at the same time.

Maya could only watch, and despite herself, she felt her own cheeks trembling, overwhelmed by the emotion on display.

Even Adam, who was lingering by the doorway, appeared to lose his usual macho exterior. He was biting his lip and nodding in approval, his gaze softening.

This was the moment of moments.

This made it all worthwhile.

Doing something good.

Doing something... righteous.

With a satisfied smile, Maya rose to her feet and keyed her mic. 'Scalpel One for Two. Jackpot. I repeat, jackpot. Our precious cargo is secured. No casualties.'

50

Kendra was on the hilltop, drenched from the rain, covered in mud.

She heard Maya give the all-clear over the net.

Jamal's family was safe.

It was a welcome relief.

Kendra leaned away from her sniper rifle and switched to her night-vision binoculars, which gave her a wider panoramic view of the landscape.

She was seeing activity now from the opposing force at the other bungalow to the north-west. Tangos were running out into the weather, climbing into their vehicles, headlights blazing to life, engines roaring.

Kendra watched the convoy roll out of the driveway — a technical armed with a .50 calibre machine gun in the rear bed, followed by a regular pickup truck, followed by another technical.

Kendra spoke into her throat microphone, 'I really, really hate to be the bearer of bad news here. But you know that other *jihadi* unit? They obviously heard all the fireworks from your end. So they're going mobile and vectoring in towards you. All three vehicles. Twelve tangos.'

Adam replied, 'Well, that sucks.'

Maya said, 'How long do we have?'

Kendra said, 'I'd say T-minus two minutes.'

Vince said, 'Understood. I've just alerted our pilot. He's already on station and inbound. Five minutes ETA.'

Kendra nodded.

They had chartered a Eurocopter from a Russian-Jewish businessman named Leonid Edelstein. He was a *sayan* — an off-the-books helper for Israeli intelligence. He asked no questions. He only knew that his pilot had to land right behind the property and pick them up.

Unfortunately, with hostiles incoming, the extraction wasn't going to be that simple.

Brushing away wet strands of hair from her face, blinking hard, Kendra worked quickly to rearrange her weapons around her. Her Arctic Warfare sniper rifle went on the ground to her left, alongside her HK416 assault rifle.

Then she reached for the duffle bag behind her. She unzipped it and pulled out two dark-green tubes. These were M72 LAWs. Disposable rocket-propelled grenade launchers. She placed them on the ground to her right.

Kendra said, 'You guys need to secure the landing zone for the exfil. I'll do all I can to delay our party-poopers.'

Adam said, 'Can you manage it?'

Kendra gave a low chuckle. 'Twelve against one. Great odds. What's not to like?'

'Okay, Wonder Woman. Stay frosty, and don't take unnecessary risks. We'll be waiting for you at the rally point.'

'Copy that. I will bug out as soon as I can and make my way over to you.'

51

Kendra raised her binoculars to her eyes once more.

She knew that her rockets had a maximum range of two-hundred metres.

That was more than enough for her to unleash hell on the *jihadis* right now.

But the convoy of vehicles was still rolling down the side street, flanked by neighbouring houses on either side, and Kendra could see civilians standing out on their front porches, swaddled in raincoats, carrying flashlights and lanterns.

Nosy folks venturing outdoors to see what the commotion was all about.

Damn rubberneckers…

That frustrated Kendra, but she decided to play it safe. She waited for the *jihadis* to reach the intersection at the end of the street, make a sharp turn, then merge with the main road.

The vehicles were accelerating now.

Their headlights were getting bigger and brighter.

Coming straight at Kendra's position.

One hundred and fifty metres…

One hundred metres…

Eighty metres…

Muscles tensing, Kendra kept her body pressed low to the ground. She didn't want to reveal her silhouette prematurely. She continued gripping her binoculars with one hand; her other hand rested on the M72 tube beside her, fingers curling in anticipation.

Fifty metres…

Now…

In one fluid motion, Kendra dropped her binoculars, rose to a crouch, and she heaved the M72 launcher on to her shoulder.

She acquired a sight picture, tracking the technical at the front of the procession.

Kendra hit the trigger, and with a shuddering jolt, the rocket ignited and whooshed out of its tube, streaking downhill, leaving a vapour trail in its wake.

The warhead impacted the hood of the technical, metal screaming against metal, and the detonation rippled across the front cab. The windows blew out, and the driver and the passenger were consumed whole by the explosion.

The sole survivor was the *jihadi* desperately clinging on to the mounted machine gun on the rear bed, flames swelling all around him. He was still alive and unscathed, but not for long.

The technical fishtailed drunkenly, its wheels locking up, and it flipped over, landing on its roof, crushing the *jihadi* gunner, pancaking him.

Directly behind, the two other vehicles in the convoy braked hard, tyres shrieking against the wet asphalt. The drivers threw their gears into reverse, retreating from the flaming wreckage.

The *jihadi* gunner on the remaining technical desperately swivelled his .50 calibre weapon around, opening up on full automatic, tracer rounds strobing and painting the darkness.

But he was confused and shooting in the wrong direction.

He obviously had no idea where the threat was.

Kendra dropped her empty launcher, scooping up the next M72, hoisting it on to her shoulder.

She had two choices now.

She could go for the regular pickup truck, which was loaded with six men. Or she could go for the technical, with the *jihadi* gunner.

Given the circumstances, it was really no choice at all.

Kendra drew a bead on the technical, knowing that the machine gun was the most immediate threat and had to be neutralised.

She triggered her rocket, sending it hissing towards the vehicle.

But the driver saw it coming, and at the last possible moment, he reacted by swerving hard to the left, and the side of the warhead scraped against the vehicle's fender, drawing a constellation of sparks, before continuing on its trajectory and detonating against a ditch at the side of the road.

Gravel and soil plumed.

A near miss.

Kendra scrunched up her face, exasperated.

That's when the *jihadi* gunner swung his weapon around in Kendra's direction. He had finally figured out where she was, and he zeroed in on her, letting loose with rapid-fire.

Kendra dropped and rolled.

She went for her Arctic Warfare sniper rifle.

Right now, she could see *jihadis* leaping from the other pickup truck, some orbiting left, some orbiting right, obviously trying to catch her in a pincer movement.

Gritting her teeth, Kendra ignored them for now.

The gunner was still the most immediate threat.

So she pressed her eye against her riflescope — forcing herself to breathe, *to breathe,* ignoring the bullets drumming into the ground right in front of her, spraying mud, chewing up grass — and she fired a single round, nailing the tango with a headshot, knocking him off his perch.

The machine gun went silent.

Kendra dropped her sniper rifle and went for her assault rifle, turning her attention to the first *jihadi* charging up the slope of the hill. He was so close that she could hear his frenzied breaths, and she could just about make out the whites of his eyes.

Only five yards away.

There was no time to properly line up her sights, so Kendra went on instinct alone, jerking her weapon up, snapping off a hasty three-round burst, just as the tango fired his Kalashnikov at the same time.

Bullets criss-crossed.

The tango clutched his throat, blood blossoming, and he pirouetted and fell.

Kendra felt a shockwave of pain in her chest, and she doubled over, gasping, wheezing, her lungs constricting like they were on fire.

Oh God…

She was only alive because her body armour had protected her. But, still, it was like being struck full force with a baseball bat.

Dizzy, nauseous, she forced herself to straighten, and she fired left, fired right, then fired left again. Her aim was all over the place, horribly inaccurate, but she managed to keep the other tangos from overrunning her.

That's when her rifle went dry.

So Kendra switched to her backup weapon — her pistol.

She fired until it locked back on empty.

Then Kendra drew a frag grenade, pulled the pin, and she allowed a full second for the timed fuse to cook, then hurled the grenade in an arc.

One, one-thousand…

The grenade exploded in mid-air, shrapnel mushrooming, and two *jihadis* were caught within the blast radius, their shredded bodies flying.

Kendra decided that it was time to bug out.

Coughing, grimacing, she reloaded her pistol and her assault rifle. She clipped the HK416 to her tactical sling. But her Arctic Warfare sniper rifle was too bulky and would only slow her down.

So she decided to abandon it, but not before stripping out the bolt assembly and tossing it into the darkness, rendering the weapon useless.

Then she spun and retreated from the *jihadi* advance, and she made a desperate dive, aquaplaning down the slope, shrubs slapping against her, stones cutting into her arms and legs.

She crash-landed at the bottom of the hill.

Groaning, she spat soil and grit from her mouth.

She thought about going for one of the electric scooters that the team had hidden in the undergrowth on the other side of the hill. But she dismissed the thought. They were too far out of reach, and moving in that direction would only put her on a collision course with the *jihadis*.

So Kendra rose and ran in the opposite direction, going for the bungalow. She could hear the familiar throbbing of helicopter rotors just ahead, and lifting her gaze, she saw a dark shape descending from the southern sky, barely visible amidst the rain.

It was the Eurocopter, in full blackout mode, coming in with its lights off.

It was her salvation.

She needed to get to the landing zone—

That's when .50 calibre gunshots strafed the ground beside Kendra, and she lurched, losing her momentum, stumbling in the mud.

Engines rumbled behind her. The *jihadis* had returned to their vehicles and were now accelerating around the base of the hill, trying to head her off. Worse still, there was a new tango manning the machine gun.

Damn it…

Blinking furiously, Kendra saw that the vehicles were gaining on her from the left.

Her only chance was the gully to her right.

The storm drain.

Move. Move. Move…

Scrambling, gasping, Kendra threw herself over the lip of the drain, sliding down the embankment, just as another burst of gunfire raked the ridge, concrete and masonry flying.

She splashed hard into the fast-flowing water below, and she ran along the canal, her legs pumping, her muscles burning.

She could hear tyres squealing right above her.

Voices yelled.

They were close.

So *fucking* close.

Kendra pivoted, aiming high, just as the pickup truck appeared over the ridge. There was a *jihadi* leaning out the passenger-side window, and she shot him, sending him flailing, and she shot the driver through the windscreen as well.

The truck swerved out of control and hurtled towards the drain.

Kendra managed to leap clear as the vehicle's frame crunched into the narrow canal, sparks shrieking as its front grill came to a stop mere inches away from Kendra's feet.

Jesus…

Kendra had barely recovered from the close shave when the technical appeared on the ridge above her. The tango on the machine gun was firing at full tilt, performing a drive-by shooting.

Kendra scampered frantically, trying to seek cover behind the wreckage of the truck as bullets pockmarked the water all around her, turning it into a violent froth. Concrete fragments ricocheted. She felt a stabbing pain in her right foot, then another whiplash of agony across her left shoulder.

Bleeding, Kendra dropped her weapon and fell to her knees, exhausted, spent.

Oh God...

The game was up.

There was no escape.

Nowhere to hide.

The technical was reversing now, preparing to make another pass at her, and the gunner was adjusting his aim. It was impossible for him to miss this time.

Ryan's face flashed in Kendra's mind, and her eyes grew watery.

She was filled with sorrow and regret.

Not being able to walk down that aisle.

Not being able to be married—

That's when something unexpected happened. A rocket screamed over Kendra's head, a smoke trail unspooling behind it, and the warhead slammed into the side of the technical.

Stunned, Kendra watched as the vehicle was lifted clean off the ground, somersaulting, its fuel tank igniting. The technical crashed back down, flames surging, and the entire chassis went up in an inferno.

Kendra gasped, the blast and the heat knocking her on to her back.

For a moment, all she could do was lie there, coughing and sputtering, her bones aching.

That's when Maya and Adam appeared on either side of Kendra, and they wrapped their arms around her, and they pulled her along the remainder of the canal, before heaving her out of the drain.

Vince was waiting at the ridge at the top.

So was Jamal. He was grinning broadly, a rocket launcher resting on his shoulder. His tone was teasing. 'Surely you did not think we had forgotten about you?'

Sitting on the soil, Kendra gave a weary laugh, grimacing as she did. 'I see that Maya finally entrusted you with a weapon.'

'She did indeed.'

Kendra gave a thumbs-up with her hand trembling. 'Good shot. Good kill.'

Working quickly, Vince used his skills as a medic to stabilise Kendra's wounds with combat gauze and tourniquets.

Then, as gentle as he could, Adam raised Kendra up by her armpits, and with a grunt, he draped her body around his shoulders in a fireman's carry.

Adam chuckled. 'Don't get used to this special treatment, Cinderella. This is a one-off.'

Kendra scoffed. 'I won't.'

They jogged towards the helo waiting behind the compound, the downdraft from the rotors creating a fierce wind that caused them to hunch over, their clothes fluttering.

The helo's loading ramp was down.

Joel was standing guard beside it, urging them to hurry.

They all climbed in, and Adam gently lowered Kendra into one of the bucket seats in the cabin.

Kendra saw that Jamal's family — Puteri, Imran and Rania — were already strapped in and waiting.

The little girl was bouncing in excitement in her seat, waving cutely at Kendra.

Kendra waved back.

That's when the hydraulics hummed and revved, and the cargo door rose and slid shut.

The helo lifted off, turbines growling, then it banked hard, reaching cruising altitude, leaving Kajang behind.

In the adjacent seat, Maya nodded as she leaned over to squeeze Kendra's knee. 'We made it. We all made it.'

Kendra smiled weakly. 'I would have it no other way.'

PART FIVE

52

The rain had stopped by the time they touched down on the private airfield in Subang Jaya.

It belonged to their Israeli *sayan*, Leonid Edelstein. He had already cleared the airspace and made all the necessary arrangements.

Adam and Kendra remained on the helo, while Maya and the rest of the group descended from the ramp, and they stood on the tarmac.

They watched as a Gulfstream private jet taxied out from the hangar in front of them. It was sleek and gleaming and luxurious. The clamshell door in the fuselage opened with a smooth hum, and the built-in stairs were deployed. Two flight attendants climbed down. They were tall Nordic women, impeccably dressed, hair perfectly coiffed.

Holding her children's hands, Puteri looked uncertainly at her husband. 'What is this?'

Jamal gave a reassuring nod. 'They will take us to Singapore. Then, from there, we will travel to our new home. Away from all this madness.'

'Is this the fresh start you promised us?'

'It is indeed, my love.' Jamal gave his wife a kiss on the forehead. 'Go. I will be with you all shortly.'

The flight attendants helped usher Puteri, Imran and Rania up the steps with kind smiles and graceful gestures.

After all the adrenaline and the intensity of the past few hours, this felt like a fairy tale. A happy ending that was almost too good to be true.

Jamal rubbed the back of his neck, his eyes glistening as he turned to regard Maya. 'I am not deserving of this.'

Maya pursed her lips. 'I know. But I'm making it happen anyway.'

Jamal sucked in a thin breath. 'My father was an *uztaz*. He made me study the Koran when I was a child. And there is this verse that still remains with me to this day. It says that if you kill one person, it is as if you have killed all of mankind. It is as if you have killed the world entire.' Jamal paused, his voice starting to break. 'I did that when I killed your father. I destroyed your whole world.' Jamal hung his head, shame written all over his features. 'I understand that nothing I do or say will ever heal that pain. And this is why I consider my own life to be well and truly forfeit. If, at any point, you wish to take vengeance on me, I will gladly accept it. I only ask that my family be spared and allowed to live in peace…'

Maya stared at Jamal. She pressed her nails into her palms, feeling years of anger and sorrow and frustration, all compressed and distilled into this singular moment.

It was so easy to fall over the edge. So easy to lose herself in the darkness. But now she felt something else too, like a warm tide rising and engulfing all the other negative emotions.

Mercy.

Empathy.

Forgiveness.

Maya swallowed, her jaw flexing. 'You know, I have a friend who's a religious scholar as well. He's a Sufi. His name is Abraham Khan. And, according to him, the Koran also says that if you save one life, it's as if you have saved the whole of mankind.' With a tight smile, Maya withdrew the photograph of Jamal's family from her pants pocket. She reached for Jamal's hand and slipped it into his grasp, returning it to him. 'I gain nothing from taking you away from your family. They need you.'

Jamal raised his gaze, wincing. 'I still want to atone for the wrongs I have done…'

'You can and you will.' Maya gestured at Vince and Joel, who were standing close by. 'Just give the Mossad all the intel that you have — weapon caches, safe houses, supply routes, troop movements. *Everything.* Help us stop the Wahhabis. Help us end this war.'

'Indeed.' Jamal nodded slowly. 'Indeed, I shall. Once I was blind, but now I see.'

'You are on the right side of history now. My best wishes to your family.'

'We will never forget what you have done for us.'

'Make this sacrifice count, Jamal.'

'*Terima kasih.*'

'*Sama-sama.*'

And with that, Vince and Joel escorted Jamal on to the plane.

The stairs rose and folded up, the door shutting.

Maya stood watching as the Gulfstream rolled down the runway, then accelerated with engines purring, lifting off, disappearing into the sky.

Maya exhaled, feeling like a weight had been lifted off her shoulders.

It was done.

53

At daybreak, they returned to the American embassy.

Adam accompanied Kendra as she was wheeled into the infirmary, where her wounds were treated.

Meanwhile, Maya met Chief Lucas Raynor in the SCIF. She calmly gave him an after-action report of the last twelve hours.

By the end of it, Raynor was so angry that his face was flushed, and his nostrils were flaring. *'Christ Almighty.* I can't believe that you actually handed Jamal Sidek over to the Israelis without consulting me.'

'It's because I knew you would say no if I asked.'

'Damn right I would have. Securing him as a high-value detainee would have been an intelligence coup for the CIA.' Raynor snapped his fingers in irritation. 'I mean, you had him. You had the son of a bitch. Why on earth did you have to cut a deal with the Mossad?'

'They had skin in the game. They deserved to get something out of it.'

'Oh, really? *Really?* Is that all it was? Quid pro quo?'

Maya cleared her throat and shrugged. 'I still consider this a win, sir. The United States has control of a key Shiite asset — Khadijah. And now Israel has control of a key Sunni asset — Jamal Sidek. And maybe, just maybe, the CIA and the Mossad can get together for a soiree and compare notes when the time is right.'

Raynor grunted and stood, pushing his chair back with a violent squeak. He started pacing about the room, rubbing his beard. 'If I didn't know any better, I'd say that it feels like you're trying to protect Jamal.'

'Okay. Maybe I am.'

'Why?'

Maya chewed on her lip, leaning back in her chair. She raked her hands through her hair, gazing at the ceiling. Then she looked back down, her expression furrowing. 'I saw his family. And I saw a chance for them to have a different life. A better life. Away from all this bullshit.' Maya made a sweeping motion with her hand. 'I mean, Sunnis killing Shiites. Shiites killing Sunnis. It's tearing the country apart. And what about us? All our political machinations? We've been making things worse instead of better.'

'We're not a charity, Maya.'

'Never said we were. But amidst the fog of war, we ought to have some moral clarity every once in a while.'

'I get it. You don't like the fact that we're being forced to work with a corrupt Sunni regime. And you desperately want to change things. But do you honestly think that this is the best way to go about it? Get real. You can't save the world, Maya. No amount of hoping and wishing is going to magically fix the problems and issues we have to deal with.'

'Maybe I can't save the world. Maybe I can't save everyone. But I can start by doing something good for one family.' Maya sucked in a breath through her teeth and gave a small nod. 'Imran and Rania will get the chance to attend a school where they can have a fixed schedule with regular friends. And they never have to look over their shoulders and worry. Isn't that worth it, sir? Isn't that worth everything?'

Raynor folded his arms. He arched his eyebrows and gave a sardonic chuckle. 'You're a hopeless romantic, Maya. Just like your father, Nathan. I can remember how astoundingly noble he could be, even at the worst of times.'

'I guess I'll take that as a compliment, sir.'

Raynor heaved a sigh as he made for the door. 'Right. Now, if you'll excuse me…'

Maya frowned. 'Where are you going?'

'To get my techs in the TOC to scrub all the surveillance footage from Bukit Bintang. Erasing all traces of your involvement in what happened there. It's the least I can do to cover your ass.'

Maya blinked, surprised but grateful. 'Thank you for your understanding, sir.'

Raynor wagged his finger. 'Ugh. I'm not doing this for you. I'm doing this for Nathan. Despite it all, I think your father would have been proud of you. And me? Well, I don't agree with your methods one bit. But I'll tolerate them anyway. You chose to stand for something moral, and that's not the worst thing to do in this mad and cruel world of ours. Let's leave it at that, shall we?'

Raynor stepped out of the SCIF, the door making a whoosh and a thunk, like an airlock.

Maya just sat there for a moment, allowing herself a smile, knowing that she had succeeded in winning the chief over. That wasn't something that happened very often.

54

It was noon when Maya stepped into Lot 10 Hutong.

It was a massive food court packed with dozens of vendor stalls, narrow alleyways and hundreds of dining tables. The lunchtime crowd here was bustling, and the air was thick with the intoxicating smell of stir-fried Chinese cuisine.

Maya found Farah seated at a table at the far end, hunched over a meal of *char kway teow*.

Maya slid into the chair beside her.

Farah didn't even acknowledge Maya. Raising her spoon and chopsticks to her mouth, she slurped her noodles casually and smacked her lips, offering the challenge, 'The rain in Spain falls mainly on the plain...'

Maya didn't bother with the countersign. She just leaned in close and slapped her palm on the tabletop, making Farah's plate jump, spilling sauce. 'Let's cut the preamble, okay?'

Farah sighed. She set her utensils down and unfolded a napkin, dabbing at the spilled sauce. 'As you wish, my dear.'

'You sent me after Omar Badawi at the Celsius Club, knowing full well that Jamal Sidek would be there at the scene, ready to take him out.'

'Mm. I am glad to see that you have caught on quickly.'

'But what is unclear to me is how you could have known about that scenario ahead of time. And how you managed to magically show up there at all.' Maya paused, frowning.

'Unless... you were somehow responsible for engineering the whole thing.'

Farah turned to look at Maya for the first time, wearing a wry smile. 'Ah. I see. You are confused by the situation...'

'Really not in the mood for *masak-masak* games right now. Tell me the truth. Give it to me straight.'

'Very well. I shall enlighten you. My endgame was simple — Jamal had to be removed from the equation. But we were getting nowhere with chasing him all over the country. So... I had to devise a way to make him come to us.'

Maya's eyes crinkled, and the dime dropped. She suddenly understood the meaning behind Farah's words. 'It was you. You spread misinformation that Badawi was a traitor.'

Farah shrugged and flicked her hand dismissively. 'You overstate my role. All I did was plant some seeds here and there along my network of agents and informers...'

'You knew that the Wahhabis would be provoked into a response. And they would dispatch their best shooter to punish Badawi.'

'Well, of course, the best predictor of future behaviour is past behaviour, as the Americans are so fond of saying.'

'And you used that to steer me right into Jamal's path.'

'Yes, indeed.'

'You played me.'

'So what if I did? I gave you what you wanted. I delivered the man who murdered your father into your hands.' Farah scoffed. 'What I could not have anticipated, however, was that you decided to capture the Butcher of Kajang instead of executing him outright.' Farah paused. 'Which is a pity. That monster would have been better off dead.'

Maya leaned back and inhaled. 'I'm sorry to disappoint.'

'What is even more intriguing is the persistent rumours that have reached my ears.

'Oh, which ones?'

'That you are responsible for liberating Jamal Sidek's family from a safe house deep in Sunni territory. And you have since handed them all over to the Israelis. They are being placed into a witness-protection programme...'

'Oh. That. Well, I can neither confirm nor deny those rumours.'

Farah raised her eyebrows, smirking as she did. 'Hm. You truly are Nathan Raines' daughter. Idealistic and honourable to a fault.'

'Yeah. Yeah, that's what everyone keeps telling me. Over and over.'

'Well, no matter. The Butcher is removed from the equation now. My *fedayeen* comrades are safer without his presence on the battlefield. And I suppose this is a satisfactory result.'

Maya nodded. 'Now I have a favour to ask from you.'

Farah tilted her head. 'Which is...?'

'With Jamal out of the picture, can I have your word that you won't attempt to track him down?'

Farah pushed her plate back and considered it. 'We Shiites have long memories.'

'As do I. But if I can learn to forgive and forget, maybe you can too.'

'Mm. Very well. Let us make a deal, you and I? So long as the Butcher stays away from Malaysia, we will have no reason to pursue him or his family. You have my assurance.'

'Okay. I will hold you to that.'

'I expect that you will.' Farah stood, then hesitated. 'Do you remember how we talked about the nature of miracles when we first met in Rawang?'

Maya narrowed her eyes. 'Yes. And I remember telling you that divine intervention really isn't my thing.'

'You should reconsider. What you did for Jamal and his family is divine.'

'Is it?'

'More than you can possibly know. *Selamat tinggal.*'

Farah stepped away, and Maya could only watch as the woman drifted through the lunchtime crowd, melting away.

55

Maya departed the Lot 10 complex, hitting the pavement.

All around her, the traffic was gridlocked and noisy.

The city smog was as horrible as it always was.

But, somehow, Maya barely noticed any of that.

All she knew was that she had a newfound lightness in her soul and a spring in her step. Her mood had changed for the better.

Maya performed a surveillance-detection run for two blocks before slicing past a corner, approaching a Toyota sedan waiting by the sidewalk.

She popped open the passenger side door and climbed in.

Adam was at the wheel, while Kendra was in the back seat, bandaged up with her arm nestled in a sling.

Adam tipped his chin as he pulled away from the kerb, merging into traffic. 'How did it go?'

Maya broke into a broad smile. 'It was great. Farah proved to be surprisingly agreeable.'

Kendra said, 'No grudges?'

'None whatsoever.'

Adam said, 'Fantastic.'

Maya turned in her seat and looked at Kendra. 'What about you? How are you holding up?'

Kendra contorted her face in mock horror. 'Poor old me? Just pissed that the wedding will have to be postponed. But

Ryan is being a champ about all this. He understands. He's just glad that I'm in one piece.'

Maya laughed. 'Well, we'll all be home soon enough.'

'Uh-huh. Going home. With Maya Raines as my maid of honour. Can't wait…'

NOTE FROM THE AUTHOR

Hello there. John Ling here. I hope you've enjoyed reading my story as much as I've enjoyed writing it.

Hey, can I ask you for a small favour? Would you like to write an honest review of my book? Let me know if the story has touched you in a special way?

The reason I ask is because only 1% of readers ever do a review.

Only 1%. Imagine that!

Yeah, I know it's a long shot, but I'm hoping there's a chance you might belong to that 1%. What I like to call a One-Percenter. The kind of reader I love. :)

Your review doesn't have to be long.

Just a sentence or two will be great.

Your feedback is precious. It encourages me. Helps me to do better.

Thank you so much for your kindness and generosity.

I look forward to hearing from you!

Cheers. :)

ABOUT THE AUTHOR

John Ling is the author of international thrillers that have appeared on the USA Today and Amazon bestseller lists.

He was born and raised in Malaysia. He now lives in New Zealand. His exotic cultural background, straddling East and West, informs his storytelling.

You can find out more about him and his work at johnling.net

Printed in Poland
by Amazon Fulfillment
Poland Sp. z o.o., Wrocław